"I Don't Have Casual Affairs, And We Both Know That's All This Could Ever Be."

Colin's arms tightened around her. "I know. And I'm sorry. I wish it could be otherwise."

Scarlett turned to him. "You've nothing to be sorry for."

Colin searched her face as she stood there. He couldn't remember ever wanting a woman more— or when he'd made a mistake as big as pulling her into his arms.

"You're so wrong," he whispered, too low for her to hear. He did have something to be sorry for. For the first time in his life, he was truly sorry he couldn't offer a woman—that he couldn't offer *this* woman—what she needed....

D0286547

Dear Reader,

A book from Joan Hohl is always a delight, so I'm thrilled that this month we have her latest MAN OF THE MONTH, *A Memorable Man*. Naturally, this story is chock-full of Joan's trademark sensuality *and* it's got some wonderful plot twists that are sure to please you!

Also this month, Cindy Gerard's latest in her NORTHERN LIGHTS BRIDES series, *A Bride for Crimson Falls,* and Beverly Barton's "Southern sizzle" is highlighted in *A Child of Her Own.* Anne Eames has the wonderful ability to combine sensuality and humor, and *A Marriage Made in Joeville* features this talent.

The Baby Blizzard by Caroline Cross is sure to melt your heart this month—it's an extraordinary love story with a hero and heroine you'll never forget! And the month is completed with a sexy romp by Diana Mars, *Matchmaking Mona*.

In months to come, look for spectacular Silhouette Desire books by Diana Palmer, Jennifer Greene, Lass Small and many other fantastic Desire stars! And I'm always here to listen to your thoughts and opinions about the books. You can write to me at the address below.

Enjoy! I wish you hours of happy reading!

Lucia Macro

Lucia Macro
Senior Editor

Please address questions and book requests to:
Silhouette Reader Service
U.S.: 3010 Walden Ave., P.O. Box 1325, Buffalo, NY 14269
Canadian: P.O. Box 609, Fort Erie, Ont. L2A 5X3

CINDY GERARD
A BRIDE FOR
CRIMSON FALLS

SILHOUETTE *Desire*®
Published by Silhouette Books
America's Publisher of Contemporary Romance

If you purchased this book without a cover you should be aware
that this book is stolen property. It was reported as "unsold and
destroyed" to the publisher, and neither the author nor the
publisher has received any payment for this "stripped book."

This book is dedicated to the "Kabby Krew":
Carol (Ben), Carole (Sparky), Denise (Tunes),
Karen (Sticks), and Sue (Bear Bait). Here's to past
"perdicaments," present plans, and future foolishness—and
many more summer vacations together at Kamp Toga.

Your Captain

 SILHOUETTE BOOKS

ISBN 0-373-76076-0

A BRIDE FOR CRIMSON FALLS

Copyright © 1997 by Cindy Gerard

All rights reserved. Except for use in any review, the reproduction
or utilization of this work in whole or in part in any form by any
electronic, mechanical or other means, now known or hereafter
invented, including xerography, photocopying and recording, or in
any information storage or retrieval system, is forbidden without
the written permission of the editorial office, Silhouette Books,
300 East 42nd Street, New York, NY 10017 U.S.A.

All characters in this book have no existence outside the imagination of
the author and have no relation whatsoever to anyone bearing the same
name or names. They are not even distantly inspired by any individual
known or unknown to the author, and all incidents are pure invention.

This edition published by arrangement with Harlequin Books S.A.

® and TM are trademarks of Harlequin Books S.A., used under license.
Trademarks indicated with ® are registered in the United States Patent
and Trademark Office, the Canadian Trade Marks Office and in other
countries.

Printed in U.S.A.

Books by Cindy Gerard

Silhouette Desire

The Cowboy Takes a Lady #957
Lucas: The Loner #975
*The Bride Wore Blue #1012
*A Bride for Abel Greene #1052 .
*A Bride for Crimson Falls #1076

*Northern Lights Brides

CINDY GERARD

If asked "What's your idea of heaven?" Cindy Gerard would say a warm sun, a cool breeze, pan pizza and a good book. If she had to settle for one of the four she'd opt for the book, with the pizza running a close second. Inspired by the pleasure she's received from the books she's read and her longtime love affair with her husband, Tom, Cindy now creates her own warm, evocative stories about compelling characters and complex relationships.

All that reading must have paid off, because since winning the Waldenbooks Award for Best Selling Series Romance for a First-Time Author, Cindy has gone on to win the prestigious Colorado Romance Writers' Award of Excellence, *Romantic Times* W.I.S.H. awards, Career Achievement and Reviewer's Choice nominations, and the Romance Writers of America's RITA nomination for Best Short Contemporary Romance.

NORTHERN LIGHTS
Brides

Northern Minnesota is a land of sparkling glacial lakes and forests that stretch as far as the eye can see. Fortunately, civilization has not yet marred its remote and intrinsic beauty. In any given spot, on any given lake, images of free-spirited Indian warriors riding spotted ponies through the tree line come unbidden, as the past collides with the present.

Shadows of turn-of-the-century French fur traders and hardworking loggers weave like the wind through the pine. At night, in a secluded bay, when the moon dances on the water and the stars shimmer in an inky sky, the Aurora Borealis mystifies, intensifying the sense of wonder in this very special place.

Come with us to Legend Lake, where its people are as in tune with the North Country's uncompromising beauty as they are enmeshed in the past. And like many before them, become enamored by the mystery of the Northern Lights.

Experience the beauty, and live all three captivating romances in the NORTHERN LIGHTS BRIDES TRILOGY as they unfold.

Prologue

With a defeated sort of longing, Scarlett Morgan let her gaze drift lovingly around the once elegant, but now sadly shabby, dining room of the Crimson Falls Hotel. "I don't know why I let you talk me into this."

"Hey, you asked for ideas," her friend J. D. Hazzard reminded her defensively. "All I did was deliver."

"Yeah, well, asking was my first mistake. Listening was my second." She shook her head, disgusted by her lack of foresight. "A raffle was one supremely lousy idea."

"It was a *desperate* idea," J.D. said. "And it worked," he added, doing his best to look affronted. He slumped back in an ancient oak chair and snagged a sweating glass of lemonade from the top of an equally antiquated round oak table—one of a dozen that graced the threadbare carpet covering the uneven surface of the hotel's dining room floor. "You needed money to keep the hotel going. The raffle provided it. The corporations who bought the losing tickets got the tax write-off they wanted. The lucky winner got the same, plus a piece of an historic hotel. And ultimately you got the forty grand you needed. Everybody won."

Beside him, J.D.'s wife, Maggie, nursed her own lemonade and shared his worry over Scarlett. He sent a pleading look her way. *Dive in any time the spirit moves you, sweetheart...like now,* his harried frown implored.

Before Maggie could toss in a bid to settle her down, though, Scarlett revved up again.

"If everybody won, why do I feel like the big loser?" She waved the letter she'd just received under J.D.'s nose. The ominous mail had arrived by boat yesterday informing her that the winner of the raffle— aka her new *partner,* Colin Slater—would be arriving in Northern Minnesota tomorrow from New York.

"Just listen to this." She scanned the letter, then read an excerpt aloud to underscore how offensive she found it. "'I'll arrive on the fifth to spend some time in residence.'

"In *residence,*" she sputtered, her temple flaring as hot as the July sun beating down on the hotel's red-shingled roof. "Like he's some land baron lording it over his peasants. Good night, J.D.! What possessed you to sell a ticket to this joker? He may be your friend, but he sounds like a prize pain in the—"

"Whoa," J.D. protested with a scowl. "Colin's a good guy or I never would have let him in on the raffle. Come on, Scarlett, you can't blame him for wanting to check out his investment."

She pitched the letter onto the table. "He sounds like some potbellied, cigar-smoking, boardroom baby boomer who can quote the Dow Jones like a rosary and plan a corporate takeover like Stormin' Norman can orchestrate a frontal assault. But I'd bet my dwindling bankroll he knows nothing about what it takes to run a hotel—especially one as unique as Crimson Falls."

"It was your dwindling bankroll that prompted you to hold the raffle in the first place," J.D. reminded her carefully. "And do I dare mention that you didn't know anything about running a hotel when you packed up, lock, stock and barrel and moved from St. Paul to the northwoods to buy it six years ago? That didn't stop you from trying it, anyway."

Beside him Maggie cringed.

Scarlett narrowed her eyes. "Is that your tactless little way of informing me it was because I didn't know anything about the business that it's buried in red ink?"

"Scarlett," Maggie cut in, running interference. "J.D. wasn't implying that your management skills have anything to do with your financial bind. He simply meant to point out that your finances are dangling by a shoestring here."

Maggie paused, her voice softening as grim acceptance cooled the anger in Scarlett's eyes. "He meant to remind you," she went on, gently reinforcing her point, "that you ran the raffle because you needed money to keep Crimson Falls going, *and* that even though Slater's business is extremely lucrative, he still paid big bucks for his ticket. It's only logical he'd want to check out his investment."

"But coming here wasn't part of the deal," Scarlett

insisted stubbornly. "He was *not* supposed to poke his nose into my business. He's a city dweller. This is the deep woods. Who'd have thought he'd bother to make an appearance."

"You'd just as well face it, sweetie. The man has a right," J.D. said, feeling bolstered by his wife's support. "Don't you glare at me, *Ms.* Too-Proud-for-Her-Own-Good. This all could have been avoided."

Blinking back unexpected tears of frustration, Scarlett turned her back on her friends. She walked to the picture window that offered a breathtaking view of Crimson Falls in the distance, the watershed that had given the hotel its name.

Yes, she could have avoided this hassle. J.D. and Maggie had offered to float her a loan big enough to cover the renovations and operating capital she needed to put her huge, old white elephant in order. And yes, she knew they had the money to do it. Between J.D.'s prosperous air freight business and the mint Maggie had earned as one of the most sought-after models in the fashion industry, the money they offered her wouldn't have made a dent in their amassed revenues.

"I may be desperate," she admitted with the prideful defiance J.D. had pointed out, "but I will *not* leach off my friends. Not even if it means I might lose Crimson Falls."

"Scarlett." J.D. walked up behind her. He and Maggie had fought this fight with her a hundred times. A hundred times they'd lost. Placing his hands on her slim shoulders, he turned her to face him. "It's going to be all right."

She stared at the floor between them, then angled a softly smiling Maggie a weary look. Giving up, she

linked her arms around J.D.'s waist and leaned into
his companionable hug. He was a good friend. So was
Maggie. No matter how many times she saw them
together—Maggie with her sleek, classic beauty and
J.D. with his blond good looks and lumberjack height
and build—Scarlett was always taken with how stunning and how right they looked together. The love
they shared also reminded her of all she'd never found
in a relationship. Of all that had been lacking in her
ten-year marriage to a control freak who had yet to
figure out he'd let a good thing go when he'd left her
and their daughter, Casey, six years ago.

"Too bad you don't have a clone, hotshot," she
said against the warmth of J.D.'s chest. "The world
could use a few more good men like you."

"Exactly what I was telling Maggie last night," he
said, deadpan.

"And the night before," Maggie put in, joining
them by the window and slanting her handsome husband an indulgent smile. "Give Colin a chance, Scarlett. I don't know him as well as J.D. does, but if he
says Colin's okay, I'd take it to the bank. And remember, he did take a chance on you."

Scarlett slipped out of J.D.'s brotherly embrace and
drew in a bracing breath. "I know you're right," she
said, and wished her heart was in the admission. The
sad truth, however, was that she was afraid. Next to
Casey, the hotel was the most important thing in her
life. It may not be much by some people's stan-
dards—fifteen guestrooms, a sometimes leaky roof
and sagging floors—but she didn't want to lose it.
Worse than losing it, was the prospect of losing control of it. She'd given up control only once in her life.
That mistake had cost her more than a failed mar-

riage. It had cost both her pride and her independence, and had taken her the last six years to recover. Now Slater's interference in her life, coupled with Dreamscape Development's plans to tear up the forest and erect condos near the falls—yet one more thing she had no control over—threatened her peace of mind again.

"I promise I'll give him a chance," she conceded. "But so help me, if he comes in here with a briefcase full of quality-management, profit-margin breakdowns and wants to turn Crimson Falls into a five-star hotel, he's going to find himself *accidentally* dunked in the drink."

An hour later, as Scarlett watched the Hazzards fly off to their summer cabin across the clear glacial waters of Legend Lake in J.D.'s float plane, she took small pleasure in visualizing shoving Mr. Colin Stuffed-Shirt Slater off the end of the dock.

It turned out, though, that even the small pleasures were going to be denied her. The boat bringing her new partner radioed ahead the next day. When it docked late in the afternoon she was waiting on the hotel's porch steps.

Roughly two city blocks separated the hotel from the new dock and the lakeshore. At that distance she couldn't make out the features of the man wearing a dark suit and a loosely knotted tie, but as he placed one foot gingerly onto the long wooden dock, she knew it had to be Slater.

When the boat rocked in its own wake, the unexpected motion caught him off balance. Suspended between solid footing and the swaying boat, he slipped, stumbled, and with a flailing grab at thin air, fell over backward into the bay.

Her spirits rose marginally as he went under with a thrashing splash and a gurgled, "I can't swim!"

She shook her head. If it took him over ten seconds to figure out he was "not swimming" in less than four feet of water, he wasn't worth the effort of saving.

"Hi, sweetheart," she said, when Casey joined her on the steps.

A gleeful grin tilted up one corner of her fifteen-year-old daughter's mouth as she, too, watched Slater flounder around like a beached whale. "Is that Mr. Money?"

"'Fraid so." Scarlett turned her attention back to Slater with a mixture of amusement and weary acceptance. "Do me a favor, will you, hon? Go fish our new partner out of the lake. But be slow about it, would you? It's a hot day. Let the man have his fun in the water."

With a last, long-suffering look, she walked back into the hotel, to see if her guests were okay, and prayed she had the strength to get through this.

One

Colin Slater trudged alongside his pint-size rescuer, doing his best to ignore both her smirk and the squishing sound his imported Italian loafers made with every step he took.

"You sure you're okay?"

Had there been less amusement and more concern in her tone, he might have assured her that he was just dandy. Had he been less humiliated about losing his footing and then realizing the water was waist-deep, he might have responded with more than a grunt.

Instead, the best he could do was heft his suitcase into a firmer grip and plod on up the lane beside her.

The teenager sent a quick, grinning peek his way. Under other circumstances he might have found her youthful lack of guile charming. Other circumstances being anything but what they were right now.

He sneezed loudly as his sinuses rejected the last of the lake water he'd inhaled in his unscheduled baptism.

Damn, he was happy to be here. About as happy as if he'd been stranded in the middle of the Mojave in a sandstorm. Barefoot. Without a camel. Or a fax.

"I'm Casey, by the way," the girl said, introducing herself belatedly. "My mom was beginning to think you weren't going to show up."

"I should be so lucky," he grumbled under his breath. Had it been his call, he wouldn't have been anywhere near this backwater lake that wasn't anywhere near *anywhere*. He'd still be in Manhattan, probably closing the Lawton deal he'd been working on for the past three months.

But it hadn't been his call. That fact rubbed against the grain with the same irritation as his soaked socks, which were slowly crawling down his heels inside his shoes.

He turned his glare on the little strawberry blonde at his side, but gave it up when she flashed that full-of-herself grin again. Becky Thatcher with an attitude. He shook his head as she pulled ahead of him and loped up the steps leading into what he'd concluded was his new business venture.

He scanned the aged and deteriorated structure he'd glimpsed from a distance when the boat had docked, then let out a deep breath. Some business venture.

It was also proof positive that Colin Slater, self-made millionaire, business mogul *extraordinaire*, per the *Wall Street Journal*, was the sucker of the century.

He couldn't prevent a wry grin. J. D. Hazzard had missed his calling. Instead of making his fortune in air freight, Hazzard ought to be selling sand to sheiks.

If he couldn't convince them they needed more, they'd buy just to get rid of him. Just like Colin had bought those raffle tickets to get Hazzard off his back.

"Consider it a good deed," J.D. had wheedled with that candy-eating grin he'd used to charm everyone from Slater Corporation's receptionist to Colin's private secretary when they'd started doing business together several years ago.

"You *are* familiar with the term aren't you, Slater?" he'd continued. "Surely before you got busy becoming so obscenely rich, you did a good deed or two."

Hazzard had known exactly what buttons to push. Just like he'd known that Colin always dug deep when the calls came in, soliciting contributions for one cause or another. "What's a few grand in your scheme of things?" J.D. had added, shoving a book of raffle tickets under his nose.

It was true. The money he'd laid out for a chance at winning part ownership in this very obviously outdated and badly in-need-of-restoration hotel hadn't created any hardship.

Until now, he thought grimly, nearly tripping on a sagging porch board. Hell. He hadn't figured on winning. Even if he had, he sure as hell hadn't planned on staking any claim.

"Thank you one and all," he muttered, thinking not only of J.D., but of his brother, Cameron, who had insisted he needed a time-out from the corporate crush. Even his secretary, Edith, had been in on the plan to hustle him out of New York.

"Before you burn out." They'd bullied repeatedly. Cameron had gone so far as to "retain" a couple of strong-armed "escorts" and then stood by smirking when they'd ganged up on him this morning like a pair of marauding Boy Scouts determined to help some poor decrepit soul across a street. He'd never fully appreciated the term shanghaied until they'd bodily "assisted" him to his private jet while Cameron issued orders to go away and stay away for a minimum of two weeks.

He took a long look around him, wondering if the only way in or out was by boat or plane. Well, he was definitely *away*. Water. Trees. Rock. Sky. That pretty well summed it up.

This wasn't just a time-out. It was a washout.

Scarlett set the bowl of chocolate frosting on the counter with a thud. "You did *what?*"

"I gave him Belinda's room," Casey repeated, sounding way too pleased with herself. She snitched a fingerful of frosting, then with a giggle, scooted out of her mother's reach when Scarlett playfully swatted her hand away.

"You've got a mean streak in you, child." Pastry knife in hand, Scarlett put the final touches on the chocolate layer cake she planned to serve her guests after dinner. "As much as I dislike the idea of him being here, we can't leave Mr. Slater in that room. Belinda will give him the business."

Casey's eyes sparkled with mirth. "She usually does when we put a man in her room."

"Which is why we make it a point to offer it to our women guests," Scarlett reminded her with a distracted scowl.

"Come on, Mom. Don't be a spoilsport. I've missed her."

Scarlett snorted. "So have I...like a toothache. She causes too much trouble."

"But it'll be fun," Casey argued. "The guests always get a kick out of Belinda when she gets on a tear."

"Only because we work overhard to convince them she's harmless. No easy feat, considering the idea of a ghost in residence has a tendency to set people a tad on edge."

"Well, Mr. Slater didn't seem to mind."

Scarlett eyed her daughter with suspicion. "You actually told him about her?"

Casey shrugged evasively. "More or less."

She raised a brow suspiciously. "Less would be my guess."

"It's not my fault he didn't believe me." Casey grinned again. "I can't wait for Belinda to start pulling her pranks."

"A wicked, wicked child," Scarlett muttered, fighting her own grin. The possibilities of Belinda's style of harassment tickled her...so much that she wished she could give Casey her way on this one. The prospect of having an advantage—any kind of advantage—on someone as wealthy and as stuffy as Slater was hard to resist.

She set the frosted cake aside and checked on the casserole she planned to serve her guests for dinner within the hour. "What do you think J.D. would say if we subjected Mr. Slater to Belinda?"

"Oh, I forgot. They're friends, aren't they." Undaunted, Casey opened a cabinet door and started gathering dinner plates to set the dining room tables. "J.D. doesn't have to know, does he?"

"J.D. doesn't have to know what?"

Scarlett jumped at the sound of an unfamiliar male voice. She spun around, a hand to her throat, then stared in startled silence at the man standing just inside her kitchen door.

"J.D. doesn't have to know that you fell off the dock," Casey volunteered quickly, shooting him a huge, wide-eyed grin. "We were just saying we could save you that little embarrassment. Right, Mom?"

Scarlett would have taken more time to wonder when her sweet, innocent daughter had gotten so devious if she hadn't been so preoccupied with other things. Like the set of broad shoulders currently filling up a substantial portion of her kitchen. And a head of hair that was deep chestnut, perfectly styled and still damp around the edges from his encounter with the lake.

And the mesmerizing magnetism of a pair of steel gray eyes set in a face that could sell anything from bourbon to woodsy cologne to black satin sheets.

So, she thought, completely unnerved by the unexpected perfection of the package he came wrapped in, this was Colin Slater.

She drew in and slowly released a deep breath, trying to pit her preconceived notions against the picture he made standing there. Her long-distance glimpse of him had been little more than a blur of a business suit and windmilling limbs. Up close and personal, it was immediately evident that a potbellied cigar smoker, he definitely was not.

He'd ditched the suit that was no doubt as soggy as the doughnuts Geezer dunked in his coffee every morning. In its place was a white, short-sleeved broadcloth shirt tucked into tan twill trousers. Not exactly cutoffs and a T-shirt, which was pretty much standard North woods attire, but it was notably less aseptic than the suit. And it was definitive in proving there was no belly—unless it was of the washboard variety.

That unsolicited speculation caught her off guard. She had no business thinking about his midsection— or any other section of his impressive body.

"Set the tables, Casey," she said with a stiff smile. "Mr. Slater and I need to discuss his accommodations."

"Rats," Casey grumbled. She gathered a stack of plates and headed for the dining room. "It would have been fun," she added with a pout, as she set her fanny to the swinging door and bumped it open.

"There's a problem?" Scarlett heard Slater ask as she stood there, all of her visible attention focused on the gradually slowing motion of the swinging door.

Unfortunately the sound of his voice—authoritative, yet soft; curious but polite; unsettling in its sensuality—kept her hormonal attention focused on those other sections that she'd told herself she wasn't going to think about.

Except that she *was* still thinking about them. Was far too aware of them, in fact, and finally had the sense to ask herself why.

Because she'd been expecting so much…so much what? So much more of a dud? So much less of a man?

Putting on her business face, she fabricated a gracious smile and willed both firmly in place.

"Formalities first." She wiped her hand on a dish towel before extending it to him. "We haven't been introduced. I'm Scarlett Morgan."

"Colin Slater, as you've already figured out."

Unlike his return smile, which was cool but polite, his hand was warm as it covered hers, his gaze intense as he assessed her. Again she was taken with the unusual gray of his eyes. Gray, however, seemed far too generic and mundane a word to describe them. Gray sounded plain. Gray sounded ordinary. They were neither. What they were was a stunning, smoky quicksilver—and right now, they were hovering somewhere between cool reserve and open appreciation. His gaze roamed her face without apology, while hers did the same, unabashedly studying him. In her case, however, she felt like a gawking tourist, wowed by the uniqueness of her discovery.

Okay, this has to stop, she told herself sternly. The problem was that she'd never been good with surprises—and Colin Slater was definitely that.

His hand was huge and hot. And his grip was firm and strong. So was the corded muscle of his forearms, she noticed, as he continued to hold her hand in his. The breadth of his chest was, for lack of a better word, impressive. And contrary to what she'd envisioned, it seemed that the only thing his shirt was stuffed with was him, lots of him, and judging by the soft dark curls peeking above the top button, lots of them, too.

It didn't end there. The way his trousers fit over lean hips and long legs that appeared to be slightly and quite beautifully bowed did unexpected and fluttery little things to her tummy.

And so it goes, she thought in self-disgust as she realized her mind had wandered back into territory even a fool would avoid.

So he was nothing like what she'd expected from a city boy who pushed pencils and little else. So what.

Just because he was pretty didn't mean he was any less of a threat. She still didn't like the idea of him being here. She liked even less that she felt suddenly self-conscious about the roughness of her hand, tucked inside his.

Realizing belatedly that they might have just set the record for longest-recorded handshake greeting, she withdrew her hand quickly and grabbed her towel. Work at the hotel was not conducive to lily-white, silky soft skin. No matter how much lotion she slathered on each night, her hands felt closer to sandpaper than satin by this time of day.

And why do you even care if he noticed? she berated herself mentally, more puzzled and unsettled by her reactions every moment.

"You—you look a little different dry," she said, determined to get it together. When she heard how inane and hollow-headed she sounded, she felt herself flush with embarrassment. "Well, that was a true jewel of a statement. As subtle as an icebreaker. And a shoo-in for the insensitivity award. I'm sorry."

Instead of taking offense, he just shrugged. "No problem. I *feel* a lot different dry, too."

She tilted her head, a reluctant smile forming that offered a smidge of sympathy and a pinch of good-will. "You mean you're not going to spend the next ten minutes justifying what happened?"

"And then another ten explaining why it wasn't my fault I made a laughingstock of myself?" He gave a dismissive and good-natured shake of his head. "Not my style."

His style, it seemed, was to take it on his jutting, masculine chin and move on. This surprised her; she grudgingly admired his grace under fire.

He surprised her again with the sincerity and the straightforwardness of his next statement. "I know this is an imposition. I hope you don't mind that I'm here."

"Of course not," she said quickly, mimicking his polite tone, then wondering why she hadn't gagged on the words. Talk about surprises. She'd just flat-out fibbed. She minded. She minded big-time that he was here.

Lying—even a white lie for the sake of decorum—was not her style. However, she didn't correct it; in fact, she compounded it. "Crimson Falls is part yours now. Your interest is understandable."

Deeper and deeper. She didn't find his being here understandable at all. And she couldn't comprehend why she didn't know how to act around this man or why he set her on the sharp side of a very nervous edge.

Yes, she did, she admitted finally. She just hadn't wanted to believe it. It was physical. Pure. Potent. Profound.

She hadn't recognized the feeling at first, because it had been so long since she'd experienced it. She'd thought her experience with John and their divorce had awarded her lifelong immunity from the opposite sex. Apparently she'd been wrong.

It wasn't as if she never saw attractive men—although, granted, if most of the men who stayed at the hotel didn't smell like fish and look like bears when they got here, they did by the time they left. But there had been the occasional single, attractive male who had expressed interest. Their interest and hers, however, peaked at opposite ends of the scale.

So what was different about this man? Sure, he was

sleek and sexy and self-assured. Not to mention sophisticated, worldly and wildly attractive. And his
voice, she'd decided, would sound seductive reading
a weather report.

It was more than that. It was how he made her
aware of herself, as a woman who'd ignored the sensual side of her nature for too long, as a woman lacking in the social graces and sophistication a man like
him was accustomed to experiencing.

"Scarlett?"

His voice penetrated her thoughts like a splash of
lake water.

"What?" she said quickly, when she realized she'd
been standing there like an extension of the counter.
"What? Did I miss something?"

He smiled. Slow and cautious and undeniably
amused. "I've heard that those short vacations are
great."

She felt her face flush as scarlet as her name. "Oh.
I'm sorry. I guess I'm a little preoccupied. With preparing dinner and all."

She let out a big breath, reluctantly met his eyes,
which were now probing hers with undisguised curiosity, and gave it up.

"Oh, hell." She tossed the towel onto the counter
and propped her fists on her hips. Her unprecedented
reaction to him had done more than rattle her. It had
made her forget who she was and what she stood for.
She didn't lie. She didn't posture. And she sure as
the world didn't call a shovel a teaspoon. It was time
for some honesty.

"The bald truth, Mr. Slater, is that I'm preoccupied
because of *you.* I lied when I said it wasn't a problem
for you to be here. I lied when I said I understand

that you want to check out your investment. The fact of the matter is—''

"You resent my presence? You don't want me meddling?'' he suggested, walking up beside her.

Her chin went up a notch. She shrugged apologetically. "I'm sorry, but yes. It's nothing personal. It's just that—''

Again he supplied the words she hadn't quite worked up the candor to voice. "You needed my money, not my advice."

Because his conclusions were so dead-on accurate, she averted her gaze from eyes that had gone soft with understanding. She fussed at a stain on the countertop.

"You know, you're making it awfully hard to dislike you."

"Good. Because you're going to have to trust me on this one. There's no need. I'm not here because I'm interested in my investment."

Her head came up. She eyed him with doubt of the hopeful variety. "No?"

"No."

He sounded sincere. He looked the part, too. She would like to accept that he was, but if there was one thing she'd learned about men from her ex, it was that they rarely did something for no reason. Even though her opinion of Colin Slater had risen with his candor, she was skeptical that she'd come face-to-face with the exception.

"Then I guess that prompts the obvious question," she said, taking her doubt to the limit. "Why *are* you here, Mr. Slater?"

He flashed her a quick, fidgety smile then began wandering restlessly around the kitchen. "Better make it Colin, since it looks like I'm going to be stuck here for a couple of weeks.''

Scarlett had to turn in a slow circle to follow his progress. He made her think of a cat on the prowl. A big, predatory cat, his eyes alert and watchful, his dark chestnut hair sleek and full-bodied.

"To answer your question," he said, still on the move, "I'm here because well-intentioned friends and family decided I needed a vacation." The tight compression of his lips relayed pure irritation.

He stopped his restless wandering long enough to pick up a quart jar of green beans that she'd canned earlier this summer. He studied the jar, set it down with a distracted frown, then shoved his hands deep into his pockets. "I stand accused of being a workaholic. I believe the term *burnout* also came up. Oh, and *battle fatigue*—they really liked that one. In their *learned* opinions, I need a rest."

She didn't doubt the workaholic reference. The way he moved around the room, the stiff set of his shoulders, relaying his tension, spoke to an underlying energy and drive. She wasn't, however, prepared to accept his statement on faith.

"On the level? You really didn't come here intending to flex a little fiscal muscle on the hotel?"

He made a soft sound of derision. "On the level."

She should have felt relief. And in a way, she did. If what he was saying was true, however, another budding suspicion, equally disturbing, set her back on that edge she suspected was every bit as cutting as his.

"These well-intentioned friends," she began slowly. "Would J. D. Hazzard happen to be among them?"

He snorted. "Among them? He's the ringleader. At least from this end. It was his idea that since I was getting away, I should 'get away' here."

"His idea? Really." She tapped a thumb against her lips, thinking of all of J.D.'s posturing about Slater coming to check out his investment. "And you really didn't come here to change the way we do business?"

He raised his hands, palms up in supplication. "What else can I say? You're going to have to trust me on this. I have no interest in this hotel."

"I'm not a naturally suspicious person," she said, a frown furrowing her brow, "but if that's the case, why did you get in on the raffle?"

Again he stopped pacing. Again, he picked up a jar—her blueberry jam this time—and studied it with a distracted scowl before setting it back on the shelf. "J.D. said it was for a good cause. Preserving the past and all that. Historical enhancement."

"And you accept everything J.D. tells you at face value?"

He shrugged. "He's never given me a reason not to."

"Until now," she said as her suspicions began to solidify.

He turned to her, his frown deepening. "Are you saying the money isn't going for a good cause?"

Reluctantly she met his eyes. With even more reticence she voiced her thoughts aloud. "I'm saying," she began with caution, "that I think I'm beginning to smell a rat the size of an airplane—a float plane to be exact—piloted by none other than your friend and mine, J.D. Born-To-Be-a-Meddler-Hazzard."

While Slater stood there, his eyes darkening to

slate, Scarlett's suspicions became more and more clear. She and her reluctant partner had been set up by a master.

"Damn that man," she muttered. "If Maggie wasn't such a good friend, I would cheerfully strangle that blond, bad-boy husband of hers the next time he shows his devious, grinning face around here."

"Look, this is really fun," he said, sounding as if he'd prefer another dunk in the lake to this conversation, "but would you mind being a little more specific?"

Scarlett eyed him with guarded concern. "You're not going to like *specific*."

"I'm not going to like paying my taxes this year, either, but that doesn't mean I can avoid it."

She gave him one last, measuring look and decided it was inescapable. "You'd better sit down."

TWO

He didn't sit down, of course. He stood facing her, legs spread, arms folded over his chest, as Scarlett shook her head. "I can't believe I was so gullible."

She forced herself to meet his eyes. When she did, she forgot all about her intended resentment and actually felt sorry for him.

"Don't you get it? J.D. had well-thought-out and convoluted ulterior motives for getting you up here."

"Convoluted ulterior motives?"

The man may be a corporate whiz and he may be gorgeous, but he was a little too slow on the uptake to suit her. She really didn't want to put this part into words, so she decided to lead him to his own conclusions.

"Okay, he leveled with you about the significance of saving the hotel, of preserving the land and the lake the way it has been for hundreds of years. But, what, exactly, did J.D. tell you about me?''

His dark brows drew together. "About you?''

She nodded, reading his blank look for what it was. The man had no clue.

He thought for a moment then shrugged. "I don't know. That you were struggling to make the hotel work. That you were…'' His words trailed off as a shadow of comprehension slowly clouded his face.

"That I was…?'' she prompted.

Closing his eyes, he raked a hand through his hair, then recounted wearily, "He said that you were intelligent. That you had a great sense of humor. Were a wonderful cook. A good mother. A good *single* mother.''

"What?'' she asked, when his sheepish look told her he finally realized he'd been had. "He didn't mention that I have all my teeth?''

"That would probably come under the attractive part,'' he admitted with a quick, self-deprecating smile. "Damn. I'm usually a little quicker out of the gate.''

He cupped his palm around his nape and let go of a deep breath. "So…it seems our *pal* had a little more than rest and relaxation on his mind when he initiated this little retreat.''

"Our *pal* is a snake,'' she hissed through clenched teeth. "A miserable, misguided, bona fide, serpent-in-Eden snake. He is *always* trying to match me up with someone. It's been worse since he married Maggie last fall. But this—this fries it.'' She stopped, suddenly more embarrassed than angry. "Look. Up-front, you need to know that I had nothing to do with this.''

He walked to the counter beside her. "Same goes. I can't believe I was so clueless."

"It's absurd. You—I mean—look at you. Look at *me*."

Colin *was* looking at her. Truth to tell, the only time he hadn't been looking at her was when he'd been busy trying not to. And despite the obvious differences, he was liking what he was seeing.

She wasn't anything like the women he was used to, most of whom, unlike her, would never be caught in daylight without the aid of Elizabeth Arden. But J.D. was right: Scarlett Morgan was one attractive woman.

From the moment he'd walked into the kitchen and seen her and Casey side by side, he'd been struck by her natural beauty. He'd also been struggling with the mother-daughter relationship. It was an old cliché, but in this case it hit dead center: Scarlett could easily pass for Casey's older sister.

Their resemblance to each other was also quite striking. Not only was their hair the same strawberry blond, they both chose to wear it in a French braid. On the daughter it looked cute. On the mother it looked nothing but sexy. Kind of a supposed-to-be-neat-but-can't-help-looking-a-little-wild sort of sexy. Just like the sparse smattering of freckles, almost lost in the summer tan of her face, and the smudge of frosting on her cheek, which gave her a wholesome yet disarmingly seductive look. Her arms were the same glowing bronze and made him think of health and vitality instead of damaged ozones and UV rays. An overwhelming curiosity to find out if her skin was the same honeyed gold all over hit him hard and low.

Not that he'd act on that curiosity. Or on this unexpected attraction he felt toward her. As she'd been wise enough to point out, they lived in different worlds, and he was making a brief pass through hers.

That conclusion, though obvious, caused an unsolicited sting of regret to stir fleetingly through his mind. Employing the discipline that had made him so successful, he dismissed it as quickly as it came.

"This explains so much," she went on, expounding on her conclusions. "Like why J.D. wasn't here today when you docked. And why he was so busy trying to make me believe the only reason you were coming to Crimson Falls was to check out your investment. It was a smoke screen."

"Just like his insistence that I not only get away, but that I get away here," he said, adding his own charges to the list of Hazzard's transgressions.

"I'm really sorry," she said.

He had no doubt that she meant it. "It's not your doing."

"Well." She offered him a weak smile. "There is one thing. At least you can get the rest you need. If you want to relax, Crimson Falls is the place to do it."

"If I wanted to relax," he countered, not even trying to cover his sarcasm as he wandered to the screen door, looked outside and wondered distractedly at the wire fence strung in a circle around it, "I'd hire a masseuse. I wouldn't fly off to the edge of nowhere, where the only game plan is to bounce off the walls with boredom."

Even before he turned back to face her, he sensed that he'd hit a nerve. A very raw nerve, judging by the look on her face. She wasn't merely angry. She was royally ticked off. And she was something to see in that state. The most notable change was in her eyes. Warm, melting chocolate transformed to a hot, spicy cinnamon.

Another one of those unguarded thoughts breached both his reserve and his resistance. What would they look like fired by passion? The possibilities were as provocative as black silk; the desire to kindle that passion as forbidden as a broken vow.

"Crimson Falls may seem like the edge of nowhere to you," she said, all righteous indignation and feminine pique, "but it's my home and I like it fine just the way it is. I'm sorry you find it lacking."

When he managed to tear his gaze away from the fire in hers, he collected his thoughts and offered the apology he owed her. "And I'm sorry for the way that came out. I didn't mean to step on any toes. It's just that I don't appreciate being manipulated. Which my buddy Hazzard has managed to do quite easily. I didn't mean to take it out on you. It's very...quiet here, is all. It makes me a little nervous. I'm used to a lot more—"

"Noise pollution? Smog? Muggings?" she suggested with an acerbic little smile that pried a quick, self-mocking grin out of him—something she'd been doing with an increasing amount of ease ever since he'd come into the kitchen.

She had a sharp tongue and an even sharper wit. Both of which he appreciated—almost as much as her eyes.

"Excitement was the word I was searching for," he countered, realizing as he said it that, as excitement went, Scarlett Morgan had generated a little of her own. She was not the kind of distraction he'd anticipated finding out here in the midst of all this water, woods and solitude.

Another one of her soft, secret smiles had him smiling in return. "What?" he asked. "You just thought of another joke somebody forgot to let me in on?"

"Actually, I was finding a sick sort of humor in all of this. It occurs to me that J.D. went to a boatload of trouble setting us up. He had me resenting you sight unseen for interfering in my business. And that letter you wrote... Ah..." She paused, reacting to his "what letter?" scowl. "I should have known. You didn't write any letter, did you?"

He shook his head. "What was it that I didn't write in this letter?"

She waved it off. "It doesn't matter. Let's just say he managed to make you come off as a prude of major proportions and then sat there defending you and begging me to give you a chance. He was really quite wonderful," she added with a reluctant chuckle of admiration, before she sobered and gave him a meaningful look. "We can't let him get by with this."

The devious spark that lit her eyes was just this side of dangerous, not to mention irresistible.

"I suppose staking him to an ant hill would be out of the question."

She took her time considering. "Not necessarily. We'll keep it as a backup plan if I can't come up with something nastier. But I do like the way you think."

They shared a quick, conspiratorial grin. As olive branches went, it was a big one. What they shared in the aftermath of that grin, however, went way beyond making peace and delved into something risky for Colin. Awareness—of her smile, of the brown eyes that danced with humor and pride, of an unbendable spirit and a suppressed sensuality—crowded around him like a sweet, tantalizing liqueur. Tempting, teasing, playing with his senses and luring him in.

She would try to deny it, but he sensed that she felt it, too. He understood her struggle to keep the awareness at bay—was grateful, in fact, that she had the sense to. He wasn't so sure if he was capable of the same restraint.

Unsettled by the suddenness and the strength of his attraction to her, he started pacing again, determined to get some perspective.

You're talking about two weeks here, Slater.

Two weeks and he'd be gone. Now was not the time, this was not the place, and she was definitely not the woman to start something with that he couldn't finish. End of discussion.

Scarlett watched him pace, thinking that in her entire life she couldn't remember fielding such a muddled mess of contradictory emotions in such a short time span. She'd been prepared to grudgingly tolerate Colin Slater. She'd been anticipating suffering through the inquiries of a dull, fiscal mind. Instead, in addition to being unwisely attracted to him, she found herself liking him, enjoying his sense of humor.

While all of that added up to *pleasant* in the surprise department, she'd have felt a lot more comfortable around him if he'd had the doughboy body and pasty city pallor she'd envisioned. He was too handsome, too masculine, too vital to ever feel comfortable around physically.

Despite that, though, she felt an unsolicited tug of sympathy for him as he roamed around her kitchen, looking irritable and anxious and amazingly attractive in spite of it. He hadn't asked for any of this, either.

And unfortunately she wasn't finished springing surprises on him.

Intentionally avoiding contact—eye, body or otherwise—she walked to the fridge, opened the door and decided to get on with it.

"As long as we're uncovering subterfuge, I'm afraid there's another contender to deal with. Casey's also played a little trick on you."

"Well, what the hell." He sounded weary and resigned and just cranky enough to make her lips quirk upward. "Why not her, too? After all, it's hard to resist a slow-moving target.

"I'm going to take a wild guess," he went on, "and venture that you're not referring to the two times her hand *accidentally* slipped when she was hauling me out of the lake?"

That child! Scarlett thought, keeping her head down, her eyes on the lettuce she'd dug out of the back of the crisper.

"Well, you've got to admit," she said, unsuccessful at squelching another grin, "you've got a few pounds on her."

"And she's got a sly sense of humor," he suggested, but not in anger.

Giving him more points for his tolerance toward her daughter, she let go of the last remnant of her resentment. "That she does. And it's that sense of humor that leads me back to the subject of your accommodations...specifically, your room."

"Oh. Then you're talking about the ghost thing."

She couldn't hide her surprise. "So she *did* tell you."

"What she told me was that she was putting me in the most popular guest room because it's believed to be haunted. By the spirit of a soiled dove if I remember her story correctly. How did she refer to it? 'The Legend of the Bride of Crimson Falls'.''

Scarlett shrugged, accepting the skepticism in his eyes for what it was. "That would be the short of it."

"And what would be the long of it?" Leaning a hip against the counter beside her, he managed to look amused, gorgeous and bored all at the same time.

She didn't blame him for being a nonbeliever. She would be one herself if she hadn't lived in the hotel for the past six years. Like anyone grounded in reality, she'd tried to rationalize the unexplained phenomena as being coincidence, weather related, electrical failures...whatever. Finally it just became simpler to accept the possibility that Belinda—or more precisely, Belinda's spirit—was a presence in the hotel, and to learn to live with it. Whatever the explanation, living with the things that went on in Belinda's room meant never putting a man in there. It kept the atmosphere in the hotel much calmer and kept her male guests from running from the room and boarding the next boat for anywhere.

In any event, whether Belinda was or wasn't a reality really didn't matter. Neither did Colin Slater's skepticism. What mattered was getting him out of that room.

She decided to downplay the situation. "You don't really want to hear about a silly old ghost story."

"But I do. I'm a business man. I appreciate a good business ploy when I hear one. A resident ghost is good for business. That's a proven fact. There's not an inn on the East Coast that doesn't boast a ghost or two to lure the curious or adventuresome. Why not an old hotel in the middle of nowhere? Humor me. Tell me the whole story."

He wanted the story? Fine. She'd give it to him. She knew she couldn't make him believe it. Only Belinda could do that, and Scarlett wasn't going to give her the opportunity.

"The hotel was built back in the 1890s," she explained as she rinsed the lettuce, then gathered the rest of the makings for a salad. "It accommodated fur traders and loggers in, shall I say, more than overnight lodging and a hot meal?"

He quirked a brow and drew the correct conclusion. "Working girls?"

She nodded. "Lots of men and lots of money traveled through the boundary waters back then. Lots of lonely men. The hotel was the perfect setup for a brothel.

"Belinda," she continued, tearing the lettuce, then chopping fresh mushrooms and cucumbers, "was one of the professional ladies. When a big Swede wandered in one day, took one look at her and asked her to marry him, she thought her prince had come."

"But the prince turned out to be a frog?" he suggested, spinning his own twist on the tale.

"So the story goes. When the big day came, he got cold feet. He left her standing at the altar—or in this case, at the bar just off the dining room."

Though she'd told the story hundreds of times to both the curious and the skeptics, she always felt a sadness when she thought of Belinda. As a woman, she supposed, she even felt a connection.

"And..." he prompted.

She shrugged, forcing herself to snap out of the momentary melancholy. "She walked to the top of the bluffs and threw herself over the falls. Her body was never found.''

''And now she haunts the hotel,'' he deduced in a patronizing tone.

She decided to forgive him that attitude, since he really didn't know any better. ''More specifically, the room Casey put you in. It was her business room.''

''And she's searching for and seeking revenge on men in general for what her bridegroom did to her.''

Scarlett smiled, recognizing the look of a man who felt he'd just been fed a long line of hooey. ''That about sums it up.''

''It's a great story,'' he conceded. ''But that's all it is. A great story.''

''Suit yourself,'' she said agreeably.

''You mean you actually believe it?''

''Casey believes it.''

''You didn't answer my question.''

She shrugged. ''Certain events haven't given me a lot of choice.''

It didn't take much to translate the look on his face. He thought she was loony. No matter. Scarlett had dealt with nay-sayers before. No doubt she'd deal with them again. If someone could come up with a rational explanation for what happened in that room when a man occupied it, she'd buy it in a heartbeat. In the meantime her money was on Belinda, and she had to get Colin Slater out of there before Belinda started making mischief—even though Scarlett had begun to agree with Casey. It might be fun to let him experience Belinda's wrath firsthand.

''Regardless,'' she countered, when her conscience just wouldn't allow it, ''I think you'd be more comfortable in one of the other guest rooms. After dinner, we'll move you to the Annabelle. It's a little larger, and the view of the lake and the falls in the distance is better. It's also at the end of the hall, so you won't have to put up with traffic walking by your door.''

"No need.'' A spark of challenge danced in his eyes. "The Belinda will do just fine. Besides, I've already unpacked.''

"No problem,'' she breezed on, trying to ignore both his insistence and the tumbling in her tummy caused by the look in his gray eyes. "We'll just transfer your things. You really will prefer the Annabelle.''

"I *prefer* the Belinda, thanks just the same. And I don't believe in ghosts, so it's no sweat, all right?''

She studied him for a long moment, considering both his stubbornness and her reaction to him. While she'd finally come to terms with it, she still didn't like that she was attracted to him.

It stirred up her irritation all over again. Not just with herself, but with him. Why did he have to come here and then manage to make her like him? And how, with one grand entrance into her private domain, had he stirred up physical wants and needs she'd packed away with her divorce decree and wedding pictures?

She couldn't afford the complications this particular attraction could bring. She didn't have the time or the energy, she told herself pragmatically. She had too much work to do on the hotel. Add the fight she planned on waging against Dreamscape Corporation's plans to destroy virgin forest and interrupt the solitude with concrete-and-glass getaway condos by the falls, and she already had a full plate.

Frustration surfaced with a vengeance. Unfortunately for him, it looked like he was going to bear the brunt of it. She knew she shouldn't leave him in Belinda's room, but suddenly it seemed like a darn fine idea. Why not ruffle those pretty corporate feathers he wore with such confidence? Why not let him feel a little of the discomfort she was feeling? And after all, wouldn't she actually be doing him a favor? If she left him with Belinda, it was a given that he wouldn't be "bored."

In the end she justified her decision by opting to employ the golden rule of business: give the customer what he wants.

"Fine," she said with a shrug and a "Don't say I didn't warn you" look. "Whatever you want."

"You can go to bed with a clear conscience tonight," he assured her. "You did your best to dissuade me."

"It's not my conscience I'm worried about," she lied, wondering, now that the die was cast, how long it would be before Belinda made her presence known. "It's your peace of mind." And her own.

"Dinner's in five minutes," she added, before she had second thoughts. When he just shook his head, obviously amused, he sealed his fate for good. No way was she moving him now. Whatever Belinda had in mind for him, he deserved it.

"Please make yourself at home in the dining room. Casey will take care of everything you need. And if you'd like, I'll take you on a tour of the grounds and the hotel itself afterward. After all, you do have a vested interest in the property, whether you want to be involved or not."

And she'd somehow take care of her sophomoric heart palpitations between now and then.

Needless to say, she would also take care of J. D.
Hazzard for his part in saddling her with Colin Slater—if he ever had the guts to show his handsome,
devious face at Crimson Falls again.

From a corner table Colin studied the dining room
with a critical eye. He'd made his fortune in the renovation and restoration of buildings deemed unsal-
vageable by those with less vision and a more-limited
knowledge of construction. He'd seen the effects of
deep freezes on structures before, but never to the
extent of the damage on this hotel. Had it been a
prospective project, he'd have passed, marking it off
as a poor investment. He was in the business of making money. There was no money to be made here.
The renovation costs would far exceed the hotel's
worth, given its inaccessibility, which meant poor
revenue-generating potential.

Sadly, it also meant the place would bleed Scarlett
Morgan dry of any profit she thought she might even-
tually make. Not your problem, he reminded himself
coldly, and watched the activity in the room.

Though it was summer now, and July was hot in
Northern Minnesota, one hundred winters of subzero
temperatures and deep, hard frosts had caused the
ground beneath the hotel to heave, buckling the floor
in several places. To wait on tables required great
balance and even better footing in the sixty-by-forty-
foot dining room, where the worn blue carpet looked
like the waving surface of a wind-chopped lake.

He watched with admiration as Casey, with skill
and agility, moved from table to table, filling water
glasses, refilling bread baskets, busing tables. She
knew the hills and valleys of the floor like a map

maker knew the lay of the land. Scarlett was every bit as adroit at traversing the rough terrain.

He had given up trying to convince himself it was his appreciation for Scarlett's surefootedness that kept his attention on her. The fact was, in spite of his resolve to distance himself, she continued to captivate him.

Skimming his thumb idly over his sweating water glass, he tried to pin down the reason. It wasn't just that she was a beautiful woman. New York was full of beautiful women. Neither was it exclusively that she was either unaware of her appeal or she discounted it, even though her lack of self-absorption was something he found refreshing.

As he sat there, he finally decided it was the puzzle that fascinated him. Why was she up here by herself? Why wasn't there a man in her life? What could possibly compel her to isolate herself in no-woman's land, every day a struggle to keep this relic going? And what drove her to fight against the proposed condominiums that outside investors wanted to build near the hotel?

He'd quizzed J.D. in depth on that issue before he'd bought the raffle ticket. "You're telling me there's money behind a project to build condos to attract tourists and she's against them coming in? Doesn't she have any head for business? Condos bring people. People bring money. And exposure. It could only help improve her business."

"She's more interested in preserving the wilderness as it is," J.D. had explained. "I've got to appreciate her motives. There's not that much virgin timber or undisturbed forests left in the upper Midwest. This is the Rockies equivalent of the last frontier.''

"From a business point of view, she's making a mistake,'' Colin had contended, but he'd bought the tickets, anyway. If he could help save the whales he could help one woman try to save a little piece of history, no matter that, figuratively speaking, she was cutting her own throat when it came to her finances.

He had no intention of getting involved. As he watched her hustle around the room, though, he couldn't stall a sharp tug of regret. Her motives might be strong, but her weapons weren't. The money she'd made from the raffle was inadequate to save the hotel from financial disaster. And pitted against the unstoppable wheels of progress, this one small, but determined, woman did not possess near enough fire power to preserve the land and the traditions she treasured.

Not only that, she lacked the strength. It was apparent that she worked too hard, was more committed to taking care of her guests than herself. For some reason that conclusion nettled him. Someone ought to be seeing to her needs. He was certain she had them—and just looking at her jump-started a few needs of his own.

He shifted, placed one ankle over the other knee and thought about why. It wasn't that he was gun-shy when it came to women. It wasn't even that he was soured on monogamy or committed to diversity. He had many friends—J.D. included—who proved that marriage as an institution was alive and well. His parents, happily married forty years last month, cemented the concept. The honest truth was he'd just never met a woman who was as exciting or as compelling as his work. He doubted that he ever would.

Although Scarlett Morgan was a pleasant surprise and had him idly entertaining a close encounter of the passionate, but temporary, kind, he wouldn't let it happen. *Temporary* was the pivotal word here and it wouldn't be right. Not with her. The lady had *home* and *harmony* and *forever after* written all over her.

He leaned back in his chair, hooking an arm over its back, and mourned the demise of what could have been a pleasant interlude. Scarlett Morgan was as off limits as a nuclear silo. The fallout potential was in the critical range. She'd never understand that, with him, affairs of the heart had to be fleeting, because business came first, foremost and always.

Business. He looked around the dining room. Business is what had ultimately brought him here: his friends' and family's conception that he needed to get away from his; and Scarlett's need to raffle off part of her business to keep it going.

He took a quick head count. There were all of fifteen people in a dining room that would easily hold sixty. No wonder she was in financial difficulty. It was the height of the tourist season, and less than half of the hotel's guest rooms were occupied.

He made a slow scan of the room. A table of middle-aged fishermen dug into Scarlett's simple but delicious meal, laughing and boasting to each other about their fishing experiences of the day. Another table was filled with six women—mid-forties, he'd guess. They were an unlikely group for this backwoods facility that catered to fishermen and family vacationers. But like the group of men, they laughed and chattered, totally absorbed in their meal and their private jokes.

A father and his three teenage sons occupied the

final table. He unintentionally overheard scraps of their conversation and gathered they were going to portage over into Canadian waters tomorrow and canoe the wilderness area for a few days, so even they wouldn't be staying at the hotel after tonight.

All in all it was a contented, if small, group. And it didn't represent enough business to break even, let alone turn a profit.

He shifted his attention back to Scarlett. He was busy appreciating the slimness of her hips, packed into a pair of well-worn jeans, when a shadow fell over the table.

He looked up and into a black, toothless scowl, sunken in the pleated leather folds of a grizzled, ancient face.

"You'd be the money man."

The old-timer's voice was as rusted with age as his joints, which Colin could have sworn he heard creak when he slowly pulled out a chair and, inch by decrepit inch, sank down onto it.

"Colin Slater," Colin said, cautiously offering his hand.

The old man considered, with a gummy compression of his mouth, before finally raising a gnarled paw in return. He met Colin's grip with surprising strength.

"So," he said, thumbing back a ragged cap with Crimson Falls written across the bill in faded red letters. He gave Colin a lengthy, disapproving appraisal, "what's yer business here, boy?"

Three

"Geezer." Scarlett appeared at the table before Colin could respond. She addressed the aged inquisitor with a warning tone. "Mind your manners. Don't you be giving Mr. Slater the third degree."

She turned to Colin. "If he hasn't already introduced himself, this is Geezer Jennings."

As in "old geezer," Colin concluded, but didn't say as much.

"Geezer's my main man, right Geez?" she added affectionately. "Handyman, dock boy, bartender. You name it, he does it."

Colin added self-appointed protector to the list as Geezer cast a proprietary eye his way. "We were just getting acquainted."

"Good," she said brightly, then to Geezer, added, "Be good, now." She laid a hand on his shoulder to soften the admonishment before hurrying off to see to the needs of another table.

Geezer pursed his leathery lips and gave Colin the evil eye—something he wasn't used to. Instead of finding it irritating, he got a kick out of it. It was rare to be the recipient of such candor, and he appreciated it for what it was. He'd learned early on that one of the hazards of success was that people told you what they *thought* you wanted to hear, not what they really felt.

He liked Geezer's honesty, but he wasn't going to let the old boy think he had him buffaloed.

"You heard the lady," Colin warned, narrowing his eyes to stall a grin. "You're supposed to be good."

Geezer snorted. Colin got the distinct impression that if they hadn't been in the middle of Scarlett's dining room, he would have spit on the floor.

"What I'm supposed t' be is careful a' the likes of a slippery Joe like you waltzin' in here and makin' trouble for that nice little woman."

"Then you can relax," Colin assured him, man-to-man. "The last thing I want to cause Scarlett is trouble. I'm just here for a short vacation."

Geezer appeared unconvinced. While Colin admired the old man's tenacity and loyalty, he also had to wonder if Scarlett actually had him on the payroll. If so, with help like him, it was small wonder she looked so tired. She probably had to cover the old man's duties, too. That aspect of her character didn't surprise him. From the beginning she'd struck him as the kind of woman who would take in, and tend to, strays and outcasts.

Geezer's scratchy voice broke into his speculation.

"I'll be watchin' ya," he assured Colin, tucking in his chin and glaring down the length of his narrow nose to emphasize the warning.

"I'm sure you will be," Colin responded, giving the old man the respect his loyalty deserved.

When he rose to leave, Colin did the same. Geezer scowled, mumbled something under his breath about "oily city manners" and shuffled out of the room.

Colin was still watching him when Casey made a quick cut over to his table.

"He's harmless," she assured him. "Mom always says he's like an old bear marking his territory whenever he wants someone to know he cares about us and the hotel. So whatever he said, don't take it personally. He probably said worse to the IRS man when he came and did an audit last year. Besides, he's just naturally suspicious of any man who doesn't wear a baseball cap."

Colin chuckled as Casey scooted away to bus a table. She was a cute kid. Her openness was a refreshing change of pace. All her chatter about a ghost, and her thinly veiled hope that she'd spooked him with her little tale, had been charming.

He glanced around the dining room again, his gaze landing momentarily on the table of women. They burst into a frenzy of giggles. When he heard a not-so-subtly concealed "hubba-hubba" followed by another round of laughter, he realized they'd been sizing him up. One of them—a blonde with a big smile and a bigger chest—gave him a shy, three-finger wave, which sent her cohorts into another chorus of squeals and giggles.

He offered a polite, if baffled, smile and averted his attention to his coffee.

"They think you're a hunk."

It was Scarlett who popped by his table this time, coffee carafe in hand.

"And I think they had a little too much wine with their dinner," he said.

She grinned. "That, too. But I've got to tell you, they are impressed. I think you've made their vacation. Not to worry, though. Most of them are married, so you're relatively safe. They're just letting their hair down."

"Quite an assortment of guests you've got here."

"They're nice people. All of them."

"All *fifteen* of them," he clarified, then wished he hadn't.

The brightness in her eyes faded. "Yes. Well, I'm hoping to change that soon."

He wanted to ask how and what she had in mind, but felt he didn't dare. She might construe it as meddling, and he didn't want to set her on edge again.

"I'm sure you will," he said instead, and complimented her on the meal.

"It's not the Rainbow Room," she said with an undercurrent of pride he found admirable, "but it'll fill an empty stomach and taste good going down."

"*Very* good," he assured her. "The cake tasted like one my brother makes."

"Your brother? Ah. Now there's a compliment a girl can take to heart."

"Why, Ms. Morgan. Is that a gender-biased conclusion I see being drawn?"

Her cheeks turned the prettiest shade of pink. "I stand corrected—and properly put in my place. I'm the last person in the world who should be making assumptions based on gender. My apologies to your brother. I'm sure he makes a delicious devil's food cake.''

"Almost as good as yours, if that's what it was.''

Her smile was soft and friendly. "I'll be able to get away in about an hour. Would you like that tour then?''

"Sure. Why not.''

"Good. When you're finished, you can wait for me out on the verandah, if you'd like. It'll be cooler out there, and you can take your coffee with you. Or if you'd rather, the bar is through that door and to your left. Geezer makes a mean Manhattan.''

He snorted. "I'm sure he does. At this point, however, I'm a little leery of just how mean it would be.''

They shared another one of those smiles that hinted at friendship. The implied intimacy had him clearing his throat.

"In any event, I'll err on the side of caution and pass on the drink. Another cup of coffee sounds good, though.''

"That I can do.'' She topped off his cup. "See you later, then.''

"Right. Later.''

It was only after she walked away that he realized how much he was looking forward to *later,* and how long an hour suddenly seemed.

Forty-five minutes later Scarlett faced herself in the mirror in her room—and could have cheerfully buried her head in a sack! Train wrecks didn't leave this much devastation behind.

She brushed a straggling curl away from her face with the back of her wrist and gave in to a groan. In the rush to get dinner ready and then clean up the

kitchen and the dining room, she'd forgotten about
her hair. She looked like a brillo pad that had mated
with a dust mop.

Her French braid had lost any semblance of style
by noon, when the heat had coaxed strand by curly
strand to break free. The episodes with Casey's puppies—who were going to be fish food soon if they
didn't clean up their act—hadn't helped, either. Twice
today she'd had to chase those two little hellions out
of her garden, out of the boat house, then, finally,
she'd had to drag them out from under the back porch
when their pathetic little cries had gotten to her. Why
she had *ever* let Casey talk her into taking one—let
alone two—of Nashata's pups was beyond her at the
moment.

It's because she was a pushover, she conceded irritably. When her friends Abel and Mackenzie Greene
had offered Casey the puppies, she'd caved in like a
dry-rotted mine shaft. The chocolate Lab, wolf-dog-
cross pups had been irresistible.

"And you," she sputtered to her image in the mirror, "you wouldn't be irresistible to a starving bear."

Let alone to a man like Colin Slater.

She felt, suddenly, very sexless and very much like
a country bumpkin in her faded old jeans, a pink tank
top that had seen better days and grubby tennies. In
the next instant, however, she felt defensive. She had
nothing to apologize for. She worked hard and she
was proud of it. Just because she didn't have much
time for feminine fluffing didn't make her less of a
woman. Not that she wanted Slater to think of her as
one.

What then, a rutabaga? she wondered.

Losing patience with herself, she tugged her braid

free and jumped into her second shower of the day. Fifteen minutes later she'd rebraided her hair, slipped into a pair of navy shorts and a white T-shirt, applied eye makeup and washed it off.

"You don't wear makeup any other day," she mumbled under her breath as she jogged down the stairs to the first floor. "You've got no reason to start now."

Yet when she opened the screen door and stepped out onto the verandah, she had sharp and immediate second thoughts.

Colin Slater was waiting for her there. Not sitting, but, as she'd suspected, standing at the rail. Hands shoved deep into his pockets, he shifted from one foot to the other with an unconscious sort of restlessness as he studied the view.

Even unsettled, the man was gorgeous. He couldn't help it, she conceded, as she watched his profile in daylight made soft by the sun's slow descent behind the trees. His features were sharp and clean; his hair, beautifully styled, enhanced them.

Some women might consider him irresistible. Not her, of course. But some women. Women who didn't liken themselves to rutabagas. Model types, she suspected. Savvy, stylish socialites with buckets of money, expensive hair and soft skin. None of which she had.

She didn't much like this overkill of awareness she felt around him—or that once again she was so conscious of her lack of sophistication. She didn't like it, but she did know what to do about it. Ignore it. Like a bad cough when the cold ran its course, it would go away. Just like Colin Slater would go away at the end of his two-week exile.

In the meantime she'd decided to take what he'd told her at face value. He didn't have any interest in the hotel. Since that had been the biggest source of her concern, she was determined to relax around him.

For all of his wealth, he seemed like a nice man. He wasn't pompous, and when he let himself relax a little, was fairly quick with a smile. He'd also gained major points when he'd faced off with Geezer and given the crusty old soul his due. All things considered, if she could get past this attraction—which should be easy, since she wasn't sixteen anymore—they ought to get along just fine for the next fourteen days.

Resolved to make his experience at Crimson Falls enjoyable, she joined him by the rail. Though he had to have heard her open and close the door behind him, his attention remained focused on the scene beyond the verandah. She understood his absorption. It was a picture she never tired of. In a companionable silence, they took it in together.

The sloping front lawn of the hotel ran the length of two city blocks. A winding lane cut through the grass and ended where water met shore. Legend Lake lay in all its shimmering glory, shining like silver-blue foil, the surface as placid as the windless evening.

Beyond the far shore, half a mile to the east, iron-rich bluffs rose five hundred feet above the evergreen and birch forest. At the high point, a ribbon of crimson-streaked silver cascaded over the cliffs, spilling from the Minnesota waters of Legend Lake into the boundary waters of Canada and Lake of the Woods.

"It's something, isn't it?" she said, never taking her eyes from the falls.

He nodded in silent agreement. "What makes the water look red?"

"It depends on what story you want to believe."

He cocked his head, inviting her to tell all.

"If you want to go with the legend, the rock behind the falls is streaked with the blood of those who died trying their luck at running them. Supposedly the Chippewa used to try to ride the falls in their canoes. Later the loggers tried to go over them, too, in their big wooden boats. None succeeded. All died and their blood stains the rock as testimony to their bravery. However," she paused, recognizing his doubtful look. "if you want to spoil the illusion, you'll prefer the scientific explanation.

"Scientific explanation, it is," she said with a smile. "It's the iron in the rock. While it's unusual to find it this far north in the state, a particularly rich vein runs the length of the cliffs behind the waterfall. When the water spills over, and the sun hits it just right, it takes on a crimson hue."

He nodded, satisfied with her explanation. "It's very striking."

"Yes, it is," she agreed softly. "The first time I saw it, I thought it was magical."

"And when was that?"

She smiled, remembering. "I was all of ten years old. My dad was an avid fisherman. Every year we'd head north from the Twin Cities and spend a week or two at a resort somewhere in the boundary waters."

"Just you and your father?"

Again, she smiled. "Actually, yes. Mom was a city girl. She didn't care for the mosquitoes or the rustic accommodations most resorts offered. And I was the quintessential tomboy. I loved it. The fishing, the hiking, roughing it. When dad found Crimson Falls, we both fell in love. Not just with the hotel, but the land and the lake. And, of course, the falls. After we found this place, we came back here every year.''

She felt his body shift beside hers then, and knew he was watching her now instead of the landscape.

"How did you come to buy it?"

"Well, that's another story." She tilted her head and offered him an out. "You sure you want to hear it? It's even more boring than the first one."

He settled a hip on the verandah railing and made himself comfortable. His look relayed that she had his undivided attention—and that he had absolutely nothing else to do, anyway, but listen to her talk.

Feeling easy with him in a way she'd never imagined possible, she decided that nothing would be hurt with the telling. "The short of it is, after Casey's father and I divorced, I decided I needed a change of pace. I'd always lived in the city—St. Paul, specifically—and I'd never forgotten about Crimson Falls. I brought Casey up here for a weekend getaway and found out it was for sale." She smiled and shrugged. "That's all it took. It was like it was preordained that I buy it, and since I've never been one to spit in the eye of fate, I quit my job—I was going nowhere fast there, anyway—took my share of the property settlement and made a down payment. That was six years ago."

"Six tough years ago," he surmised, reading more into her words than she'd wanted him to.

Unfortunately he was also accurate. "Yes," she conceded. "In some ways it's been tough. I suppose it always will be."

"Then what is it that keeps you here?"

His question was heavy with more than curiosity. There was wonder there and a wanting to understand something he really couldn't fathom. She decided to accommodate him, although she suspected that a man as high-profile and intense as he was would never fully comprehend her reasons.

"The same thing that brought me. And more. It's the hotel. The land. The people." She shrugged. "It's a way of life I value and can't experience anywhere else."

He was quiet for a long moment. "And what is it about the life...specifically...that you value? I see isolation. Hard work. Little return for your efforts. You're smiling. Why?"

"It just amuses me, I guess—how the human race can have such vastly different perceptions of the same set of circumstances." She walked to the steps, hugged an arm around a porch column and leaned against it. "You see this as hard work and little reward. I see it as honest work, and if I got no other reward than waking up to this sight each morning and going to bed with it each night, I would consider myself well compensated."

Again another long, appraising silence, as he crossed his arms over his chest and averted his gaze toward the bay. "It's so-o-o quiet."

"You make it sound so-o-o ominous." She smiled again. "It's a little unsettling at first, but you get used to it. And then you get to love it."

He gave her a doubtful look.

She laughed. "Come on," she said, knowing the only way he would be convinced was if he wanted to be. "I can try to convert you to my way of thinking all night, but I don't think it's going to happen. Let's take that tour.''

The tour consisted of a walk around the hotel. She pointed out the fresh paint on the shiplap siding. Colin silently noticed the crumbling foundation. She extolled the virtues of the widow's walk topping the two-story structure. He noted, with a frown, the deterioration of the shingles and the rusted gutters.

Two things he could appreciate, however, were the rough, verdant beauty of the land and Scarlett's green thumb. Everywhere they turned she'd planted flowers, somehow making them grow among the rock and moss and pine—begonias, geraniums, glads, snapdragons. Patchworks of flowerbeds peppered the grounds with color and fragrance; baskets hung from the verandah's eaves; filled vases decorated the dining room tables.

Flowers weren't her only vice, as she referred to them. Her herb garden was obviously a great source of pride, as was the vegetable garden surrounded by the same single-strand wire fencing that was outside the kitchen door. He'd been curious about it since he'd spotted it from her kitchen earlier but had been distracted before he could ask.

When they got to the back of the hotel where the kitchen extended from the main body of the building, he couldn't contain his curiosity any longer.

"What's that fence about?" He nodded toward the single strand of thin wire.

"Don't touch it," she warned when he stepped in for a closer inspection. "It's hot."

"Hot? As in electric?"

She nodded. "We've had a bear problem this summer."

"Bear? As in...*bear*?"

She chuckled. "Yes. As in bear. Black bear. They're thick as thieves up here. And they're pilfering little beggars. Especially this summer. We had a fairly dry spring, so the wild blueberry crop's a little sparse. Once a week or so, a crew of them follow their noses to the kitchen and try to get inside to satisfy their sweet tooth."

"You're not serious."

"'Fraid so. A couple of summers ago a sow and her cubs broke through the screen door, ate five fruit pies I'd just baked and trashed the kitchen."

She laughed at the memory, then at the stricken look on his face.

"Don't worry. As long as the hot wire's up, they won't get in. If they bump it, it stings them just enough to scare them off. Do be careful, though, and don't wander into the woods after dark. Black bears are relatively harmless, but if you surprise them, they'll react just as a human would if they feel they're being threatened. And believe me, six or seven hundred pounds of protective bear can convince you in a hurry that Winnie the Pooh isn't the softy he was made out to be."

"Bears," he said, shaking his head. "You actually live with bears."

"And a ghost," she reminded him playfully, and grinned again when he rolled his eyes.

Casey came tearing around the hotel about that time, hot on the heels of two wildly running puppies, the bloodlines of which he couldn't even begin to guess.

"Casey..." Scarlett warned.

"I know. Keep 'em out of the garden. I will. We're going down to the dock for a little game of fetch."

As fast as they appeared, they were gone in a flurry of playful yips, galloping feet and flopping ears.

Scarlett watched them go with a shake of her head. "Oh, to have that energy."

Not for the first time Colin noticed how tired she looked. She may defend this way of life, but he could see it was taking its toll on her.

It wasn't any of his business, so he didn't comment, even though it nettled him. Instead he followed her in brooding silence when she headed back inside. She led him through the ornately decorated lobby furnished in antiques, then up the stairs to the second floor, past Belinda's room to the Annabelle.

"Sure you don't want to change your mind now that you've seen this room?" she suggested hopefully.

"It's a nice room, but not a chance."

She gave him a worried look, but didn't press, as he trailed her from room to room.

"As you can see, like the antique oak tables in the dining room, I've tried to keep the bedrooms furnished in the period as much as possible. Iron beds, washstands, oak armoires. I want my guests to experience the same setting as the fur traders and loggers the hotel was built for."

Colin had to admit there was a certain historical feel, and perhaps even a tug of nostalgia, for what life in this wild country must have been like at the turn of the century. The framed photographs of the lake land that hung in the dining room and lobby suggested that not much had changed here even into the mid 1900s. He might even understand why vacationers would like to spend a week or two here in the summer. He was still having difficulty, however, fathoming why anyone would prefer that era to the present age of technology; or the remoteness of this place to the teeming vitality of the city.

Something else had been bothering him. "I scanned some of your brochures while I was waiting for you after dinner. The phrase 'No roads lead to Crimson Falls' kept popping up."

"It's true. The only way to get here is by boat or plane."

"Then how do you get supplies? Electricity?"

She provided an explanation as she led him back to the center of the floor. "Same way...for the supplies that is. Boat or plane. We have our own generator that provides electricity. And after lights-out at ten, we only run power to the kitchen, to conserve energy. That's why there's an oil lamp in each room."

Something else had been bothering him. "How does Casey get to school?"

"Ah, well, that sometimes takes a little doing," she confessed, as they walked back down the hall, remarking offhandedly that behind them were her and Casey's private quarters.

"The closest school is at Bordertown, forty miles to the northwest," she said as they reached one smaller, central door. She stopped and unlocked it with a key from a ring she fished out of her shorts pocket.

"In the fall and spring," she said, opening the door and starting up a dark, narrow stairway, "we drive a forest access road to Vermilion Narrows. The lake's only about twenty feet wide there. We hop in a boat and make the crossing. I leave my car on that side of the lake and I drive her from there. Or sometimes I just drive her as far as Abel and Mackenzie Greene's—friends of ours—and they take her and Mackenzie's brother, Mark, the rest of the way.''

"You do this in the winter?''

At the top of the stairs she put her shoulder to yet another closed door. When it wouldn't budge, he offered to help.

She stepped aside, still talking. "By mid-December through mid-April the lake is frozen solid. Then we either drive or snowmobile across. If the weather's too bad, or the lake's too rough, she monitors her classes on a shortwave radio.''

"Very resourceful,'' he said with a grunt as the door gave way. He stepped back so she could walk around him.

As she passed, he detected the faint fragrance of flowers. A soft, elusive scent that was very female and exceedingly exotic. Just as the touch of her shoulder, where it brushed against his chest when she squeezed by him, was profoundly feminine.

This close he could see the fine red-gold hue of the hair at her nape. Still damp from a recent shower, it clung in soft, silken curls beneath her braid. The skin there looked soft, too. And tempting. He had a sudden image of his hands brushing her hair aside, his lips descending to taste and caress that secret, sensitive spot…along with many others.

"*Resourceful* fits exactly,'' he heard her say through a haze of sexual awareness. "It's another plus for living here—we're forced to be inventive.''

The sound of her voice did little to bring his erotically wandering mind back in tow. Fortunately, when she stopped and turned to him, she must have read his silence as dissension, when in fact he was still trying to come to grips with an unprecedented urge to pin her against the stairway wall and kiss her until neither of them cared about anything but the moment.

"You don't see it as a plus, do you?"

What he saw was her. Naked. Needy. Beneath him. "What I see," he managed to say, working hard to stall that vivid, provocative image, "is a lot of trouble."

Trouble started all over again when she smiled.

"There's that perspective thing again. *I* see it as being self-reliant. Too many things are too easy these days. Living here makes me appreciate what I do have. It's good for Casey, too. She has a strong sense of self."

"She's a nice kid," he agreed, concentrating on the image of Casey's sweet, youthful face to divert him from other, more dangerous images of her mother. "Do you ever feel like you're depriving her?"

"Depriving her?" Her eyes widened to relay her surprise that the thought would even cross his mind. "Here she's exposed to a variety of interesting people. She's loved, she knows how to make her own fun. She's a straight-A student. Sound like a deprived child to you?"

He had to admit that she might be on to something. Casey was unspoiled, fun loving yet responsible. She'd worked like a trooper during the dinner hour tonight. He had little doubt she was a help to Scarlett in many ways. That she was such a well-adjusted child was a credit to Scarlett and the way she'd raised her.

"No," he admitted. "She doesn't seem deprived. You've done a good job with her."

Their shoulders brushed again. In the dim light of the narrow hallway, he could sense the color rise on her cheeks. It was then that he realized she wasn't as oblivious to the attraction sizzling between them as he'd thought.

In fact, he sensed that she was having the same problem he was. Damn. It was bad enough to know that his libido was giving him fits. Knowing she was struggling, too, made it that much harder to ignore.

When she turned away and scaled the last step to the top of the stairs, he let out a breath that should have been relief but felt more like disappointment.

"And Mother Nature did a great job on this, wouldn't you agree?" she asked, as they stepped out of the stairwell and into the twilight hues lighting the widow's walk.

He agreed. Oh, yes. He agreed in spades, but it wasn't the view he was appreciating. It was the woman at his side. And it had to stop.

Four

Colin made himself walk to the rail and look down over the spectacle of Legend Lake and Crimson Falls. With effort, he concentrated on the view and grasped a tentative understanding of why she loved this place beyond what might be good for her.

In this light, soft with the coming of dusk, an iridescent translucence cloaked the air, casting the scene before them in cooling shades of blue. Even the grass, two stories below, lay like a rumpled blanket of muted, blue-green gloss; the evergreens surrounding the clearing rose in a midnight indigo splendor; the lake shimmered metallic, mirrorlike and still. And the falls, streaked with crimson and frothed with white, lent color but not conflict to the picture-postcard scene.

Only the woman at his side added discord to the peace. To his peace. Of mind and body. Her serenity beside him, as she experienced this view that was so special to her, only served to unhinge him more.

Could she really be this uncomplicated? This pure of purpose and need? Her profile was as clean and defined as the values she treasured. Her hair shone more blond than red by evening light. Not for the first time he noted that she'd rebraided it. Not for the first time he wondered if she'd done it for him.

The prospect was as appealing as it was unsettling. And absurd, he realized, when he caught himself courting thoughts he had no business entertaining.

She turned to him just as he managed to drag his attention from her to the lake.

"Bigger men than you have been struck speechless by this view."

The smile in her voice wouldn't have been there if she'd realized that it was her, not the scenery, that held him spellbound. He wondered what kind of man would have left a woman like her.

"Sometimes when I come up here, I can picture the bay the way it was in its heyday. Teaming with hundreds of men and boats, or stacked shore-to-shore with thousands of floating logs on their way to the mills in Duluth. And I can see the ladies watching from this vantage point, waiting for the men to make them laugh, spend their money, ease a little of the loneliness."

Odd, he thought, that the word *loneliness* had entered her conversation. Odd and contradictory for a woman who professed to a love of isolation. The poignancy in the statement tugged at his chest in an unfamiliar and uncomfortable way. Thankfully, before he gave in to questioning the soulfulness of her statement, she diverted him.

"Would you listen to me, waxing melancholy like a sentimental sap. It's the widow's walk, I guess. Every time I come up here, I get a little too wrapped up in the lives those men and women must have lived." She smiled apologetically. "Come on. Let's finish the tour before I make a bigger fool of myself."

As fools went, he figured she wouldn't hold a candle to him, if he acted on the sudden, impulsive desire to pull her against him, stroke a finger along her jaw and tell her she didn't ever have to be lonely again. Fortunately for both of them, the chances of him acting on that impulse were about as slim as those of her *admitting* her loneliness—even, he suspected, to herself.

The final stop on the tour took them back downstairs to the bar. Of all the aspects of the hotel, this is the one that Colin appreciated the most.

It was in this room, with its rolling hardwood floors and its beveled glass mirror and brass foot rail skirting the bar, that he could actually envision life as it must have been. Where the widow's walk had been a woman's territory, the bar had definitely been a man's.

A gaudy painting of the obligatory reclining nude, a voluptuous, full-breasted siren complete with a feather boa and a come-hither smile, hung above the gilt-framed mirror. An ancient, but working, player piano filled one corner of the room. A scarred billiard table with woven leather pockets sat in the middle of the floor. Shims, stuck strategically under its thick legs, helped keep it level. Old photos, posters and dollar bills, signed by visitors who'd passed through and wanted to leave something of themselves behind, plastered the walls in a hodgepodge of disordered memorabilia.

And then, of course, there was Geezer, another relic from the past, snoring softly in a corner booth.

Scarlett pressed a finger to her lips when she spotted him. "Let's let him sleep."

"No problem," Colin whispered back. "One more bolt from his evil eye tonight and I'm liable to turn into a pillar of salt."

She grinned and slipped behind the bar. "What's your pleasure?"

"Sarsaparilla?" he suggested, giving in to an impulse that he'd have felt foolish acting on if she hadn't played along.

"Sorry, mister. We're fresh out. How about a soda instead?"

He propped an elbow on the worn bar rail. "That'll work."

"You wouldn't rather have a drink or a beer?"

"What are you having?"

She lifted a bottle of white wine.

"That'll work even better."

"So," she said, setting out glasses, then filling them. "What do you think of the hotel, now that you've had the fifty-cent tour?"

He scratched his brow, considering what to say as she rounded the bar, slipped onto a stool beside him and tipped her wine to her lips. "It's a very unique place," he said evasively, and tried not to think of the delicate crystal glass and her full pink lips and how utterly sensual they were in combination.

"I hear a qualifier in there. Come on," she prompted when he stalled. He was still fighting his reaction to the simple act of a beautiful woman sip-ping wine. Digging deep, he searched for something positive to say.

In the end his preoccupation with her mouth was so disturbing that he blurted out his take on the hotel to vent his irritation with himself. "It's falling down around you, Scarlett."

She shifted uncomfortably on her stool. "You think I don't know that? That's why I was forced to hold the raffle."

Oh, yes, the raffle. Propping both elbows on the bar, he swilled the wine around in the glass, then downed a hefty swallow. The damn raffle was the event that had brought him here. From what he'd seen, the money she'd made from the ticket sales wouldn't be enough to cover even the cost of basic repairs, let alone make the restorations she'd told him she wanted to complete.

He didn't want to point that out to her. Not tonight. Maybe not ever. After all, even though he had to keep reminding himself, he was not involved. Not in the hotel. Not with her. He was just here to get a few people off his case, and then it was back to business as usual. He wasn't here to worry about her or to help her out of her current difficulty. Besides, she hadn't asked. To keep the appropriate distance between them, he wouldn't offer.

"Well," he said, reaching for the bottle and refilling her glass, then his. "I've no doubt you'll put the money to good use."

"You're right about that," she said with a confident tilt of her head. "I've a little Scottish blood running through these veins. I can make that money stretch a long way. And speaking of money, I didn't give J.D. the chance to fill me in. How is it that you make yours?"

She blanched, then covered her face with her hand. "Oh, my gosh. I'm sorry. I don't know where that came from."

He just smiled, appreciating her candor every bit as much as he had Geezer's. "I suspect it came from curiosity."

"Or bad manners. I'm not usually so..."

"Direct?" he suggested.

"Snoopy," she amended, and he could see that she really was embarrassed. "It's really none of my business."

"Justified is the word you're looking for," he said, wanting to put her at ease. "I'd probably be curious, too, if I knew someone had dropped money sight unseen and bought into my business.

"Renovation," he supplied, when it became apparent she was prepared to drop the issue.

She slanted him a questioning look.

"It's what I do to make my money. I renovate. I buy run-down property at deflated values, restore and refurbish, then sell for a profit."

She looked interested but a little uneasy. "Kind of ironic, don't you think? That you now own a piece of yet one more property in need of restoration?"

Now he understood her wariness. "You're jumping to conclusions again. I thought we'd gotten past that. I have no designs on this hotel—for restoration, resale or otherwise. Don't take offense, but it's way too small a project. While we started out with smaller buildings, we deal strictly with corporate buildings— multiple stories, prime business locations—that attract major players."

She took another sip of wine. Again he became mesmerized by the fit of her full lips to the rim of the glass, the gentle convulsion of muscle beneath the silk of the skin at her throat as she swallowed. The thought of the wine settling her, soothing her, had the opposite effect on him. He clenched his jaw, then methodically uncurled his fist, finger by finger, from around the fragile wineglass, before he broke it.

"I'm sorry," she said after a moment. "For slipping into that groove again. It's just that Crimson Falls means so much to me. The thought of someone—even someone who I've decided is *not* a corporate stuffed shirt," she added with a pained smile, "wanting to exercise control over what's mine, is very distressing."

Very distressing, he echoed in silence. Too distressing. Suspiciously distressing. It fostered a whole new catalogue of questions. Like who was responsible for her wariness. Who had been so controlling in her life that she felt threatened by the prospect of losing that control. Had to be the ex, he decided, as the guarded look was slow to leave her eyes.

And the ex had to be a fool, he concluded, draining his second glass. Colin knew he wasn't a marrying kind of man, but he'd seen enough of Scarlett Morgan to realize that any man who'd been lucky enough to marry her had been the king of fools for letting her go.

"J.D. mentioned something about a development company coming into the area," he said to divert his thoughts to safer ground. "He also told me you were against it."

"He's got that right."

"From a business standpoint, the condos could only help yours."

She cut him an impatient look.

He didn't back down. "Think about it. The condos mean more people. That means more exposure for the hotel. It also means more accessibility. All of that amounts to revenue."

"What it amounts to is invasion. This land is special. It's unique and unspoiled, and that's a commodity more valuable than money any day."

"A commodity more valuable than money. Now there's a concept that would blow the Wall Street moguls out of the water."

"It's a concept a few more people should think about."

As suggestions went, hers wasn't the most subtle. It was also a reminder—to both of them—about priorities. And the differences between theirs. His priority was and always had been success. Success to him meant making money. Lots of it. Success for her meant surviving and preserving both tradition and topography. Neither were endeavors he'd ever spent much time or energy contemplating.

They were polar opposites. This fact should have been enough to curb his interest.

Unfortunately, it wasn't. Her values only intrigued him more.

Colin didn't know what bothered him more: seeing through the tiredness in her eyes that fatigue was taking its toll on her, or the protective feeling that made him unexpectedly suggest that she go to bed and get some rest.

"I need to wake Geezer and make sure he gets to bed okay, before I turn in," she'd insisted.

"I can handle Geezer."

Either she recognized that his tone left no room for negotiation or she was exhausted enough not to argue. In any event she had conceded with a yawn, left Geezer to him and wished him a good-night.

That had been an hour ago. After she'd left, he'd poured himself another glass of wine and nursed it with a growing concern over the tangle of emotions one small, self-reliant woman had managed to evoke.

He tried to convince himself he was preoccupied with her out of boredom. He wasn't used to having so little to do...and so much free time to do it in. The prospect of having a blank slate for the next thirteen days added to the problem.

Generally, he had far more to occupy his mind. Whether he was in New York, working at his corporate headquarters, or out of state or abroad on a buying trip or site inspection, his days began at five a.m. with a five-mile run at the closest private health club available. He was on the job at seven, rarely called it a day until seven or eight at night, and even then most evenings ended with a business dinner. Weekends were spent on the fax or with his lap-top reviewing bids and cost estimates. He was the hands-on CEO of his own corporation, and he intended to keep it that way.

None of that made him a workaholic—not in his eyes, at least. He worked hard, yes, but that's the way he liked it. His work was his life. It grated on him that he increasingly found himself defending that position. He didn't want anyone but himself deciding how much he worked, or if the number of hours he

chose to work was healthy. As long as he didn't expect long hours from anyone else who worked for
him, it wasn't anyone's business.

After all, he was content. He was productive. What
more could a man want out of life?

A woman like Scarlett Morgan.

That unwelcome conclusion popped into his mind
before he had a chance to waylay it. And since he
didn't want to deal with why it had slipped in so
easily, he woke a softly snoring Geezer, helped the
old man to his feet and made sure he made it out of
the bar.

Alone, and unused to the quiet and the idle time to
think about something other than business, he walked
to the lakeshore. For over an hour he just stood there.

The faint sound of the falls tumbling over the bluffs
in the distance infiltrated a quiet he'd thought to be
absolute. There were sounds here—they were just different from the sounds of the city. Like background
rhythms to a slow, hypnotic dance, the water made a
soft, lapping babble as it gently mated with the shore.
From a far corner of the bay, a loon called, the cry
reminiscent of an old Henry Fonda, Katherine Hep-
burn movie his mother had been particularly fond of.
Actually, the entire area, with its towering pine and
glacier-carved boulders and moodily shifting water,
reminded him of the setting for that classic film.

Accompanying the night sounds was a blanketing
sense of...of what, Slater? he asked himself with a
scowl, as the explanation eluded him. It was something he couldn't pin down. Solitude, yes, but not so
much a sense of isolation as it was...serenity. That
was the word that finally came to mind, surprising

him. *Serenity.* And *peace.* That word surprised him even more.

Neither concept appealed to him. Well, maybe now that he was experiencing them they didn't seem so bad—just, abstract from his point of view. He'd never had the time for either.

He drew in a deep breath, let it out, then wandered onto the dock and looked out over the lake. So this is what Hazzard was always harping at him to experience.

"It's like no place on earth, man," J.D. had said more times than Colin cared to count. "It's like you go up there and a door closes on the rest of the world. You forget your ambition, you forget your drive—you forget about fortunes to be made and lost and you just *experience.*"

It had always sounded like a sinful waste of time to Colin. Until now, he realized, in a cathartic moment of truth. Until this exact moment, as he stood there, soaking up the essence of the feeling J.D. had preached with the zealousness of an evangelist, he hadn't been able to fathom the allure of not having one single, solitary thing to accomplish except appreciating the moment.

He breathed in the clean air. He felt the essence of the night enfolding him. Beneath the dock, the rhythm of the lake rocked against the wooden pilings in a gentle undulating motion. Above him, as big and vast and mysterious as these unaccustomed feelings, the sky stretched into infinity, glittering with an array of stars so crystalline and bright it stunned him.

So this was night without smog and manmade light.

And this was Colin Slater without business on his mind.

Uncomfortable, suddenly, with the ease at which he'd slipped out of business mode and into relaxation, he shoved his hands in his pockets and turned back toward the hotel.

It was late. After eleven. The hotel was dark, except, he noted with a frown of curiosity, for a light blazing from a window on the second story. Mentally he walked through the floor and realized that the light was coming from his room.

Picking up his pace, he hiked the distance to the verandah, thinking all the time of Scarlett telling him about lights out at ten p.m. He remembered her saying, "That's why there's an oil lamp in each room."

There was no way an oil lamp could generate that much light. Short of a spotlight, there was only one thing he knew of that burned that bright—fire.

Heart pounding, he sprinted up the veranda steps, jerked open the hotel's front door and took the stairs to the second landing two at a time. By the time he raced down the hall and reached his room, he was in a rare panic. He grasped the doorknob, then jerked his hand away. It was hot to the touch, the light glowing from under the threshold, beacon bright.

He spun around, searching the darkened hall. When he spotted the fire extinguisher, he jerked it free from its metal housing and rushed back to the door. Flipping the nozzle, he sucked in a deep breath and geared up to ram the door with his shoulder—just as it swung open with a slow, creaking groan.

No blazing light spilled out to greet him. No fire burned beyond the open door. No smoke hung in the air to indicate there had ever been one.

Brows narrowed, he stepped warily across the threshold into the room. On a small night table in front of the window, a lone oil lamp burned at low wick, its flame illuminating the room in a soft, golden glow. Welcoming. Inviting. Like the bed with its covers turned down.

He closed his eyes, shook his head to clear it, then scanned the room again. Nothing was amiss. His empty suitcases sat neatly in the far corner. A soft breeze stirred the curtains at the open window. Everything was peaceful. Normal. Orderly—except for the air, which seemed to close in around him like an invisible velvet glove. The space around him felt charged with electricity, pregnant with anticipation, as a movement on the far wall caught his peripheral vision.

Slowly, he turned. Mesmerized, he watched as a shadow formed and swelled, dancing across the faded floral wall paper. He stared, disbelieving, as it undulated, changing height, changing size; even, it seemed, changing substance. He fought it every inch of the way, but there was no denying that as he stood there, captivated by the motion, transfixed by the sight, the shadow took form and shape.

Slowly, incredibly, as it hovered in the pale and fading light, the shadow seemed to solidify into the shape of a woman—a sensual, voluptuous woman, her seductive dance as intoxicating as aged brandy...as enticing as mist shifting through midnight...as inviting as the sighing sound of the door closing softly behind him.

"What do you think?" Casey asked her mother as they observed Colin early the next morning from behind the partially open kitchen door. "He looks good and rattled to me."

"I'm not so sure," Scarlett said, as she watched him where he sat in the dining room at the same corner table as he had last night. "He looks puzzled, but my guess is he's busy making rationalizations as we speak."

"I figure she pulled the brilliant light and shadow dance number on him."

"That would be her usual opening act." Scarlett shook her head, guilt getting the best of her. "I'd better go check on him. And I ought to be whipped for leaving him in that room."

"Ask him if he slept with the fire extinguisher all night," Casey suggested, her amusement tinged with sympathy.

"If he slept at all."

Cutting off a caramel roll from the ones she'd just pulled out of the oven, Scarlett set it on a plate, added a couple of pats of butter and headed for his table.

She set the plate in front of him, then pulled out a chair and sat down.

"Good morning," she ventured softly.

He dragged his gaze from his cup to her face.

The dark circles under his eyes and the haggard lines around his mouth told her there was no need to ask if he'd slept well.

"I believe I tried to warn you," she said without preamble, but with the sympathy she felt he deserved.

"There's an explanation," he said firmly. "For everything."

Although he was in denial, Scarlett gave him points for not denying that something out of the ordinary had happened in Belinda's room last night. She hadn't experienced firsthand the sight of light blazing from the window, the heat-charged doorknob or the dancing shadows, but she'd heard accounts from more than one shaken male guest.

"Have you had the wiring in this place checked recently?"

"No," she conceded, giving him that straw to cling to. If he wanted to believe what happened was the result of bad wiring, she'd give him that small gift of peace of mind.

"The new dock was the priority. Wiring is the next item on my list of repairs. In the meantime, just in case it is the wiring, why don't we move you out of there today? If the Annabelle doesn't suit you, there's another room available with a lake view. I'm sure you'd like it."

"I'm fine right where I am," he insisted, and she saw in his eyes the tenacity that had gotten him to the level of success he'd attained.

To her way of thinking, though, that didn't let her off the hook. "Look. There's no need for you to stay there. You don't have to prove anything to me. Besides," she added, fabricating an excuse for him to vacate with grace. "I'd really hoped to give that room a good once-over this month. The floors need to be resealed, the windows washed—there's at least two weeks of work I've been putting off."

"If you've put it off this long, then it can wait until after I'm gone."

The determination in his eyes, and the insistence in his tone, accomplished two things. One, her conscience quit harping at her. Two, his reference to his imminent departure caused a twinge of regret somewhere in the vicinity of her heart.

Of the two, the latter was the most difficult to deal with.

It made no sense that his leaving would bother her. She wasn't even supposed to like the man. Before his arrival, she'd been anticipating his two-week stay the way she dreaded the first of each month when the bills were due.

Yet here she was, anticipating the sting of his good-bye like some schoolgirl in the throes of her first crush.

He wasn't the only one who hadn't gotten a decent night's sleep. Belinda may have been the cause of his sleeplessness, but he'd been the cause of hers. As tired as she'd been last night, she'd lain awake far too long, thinking about the fact that he'd soon be gone. Attraction, she decided, was a really rotten thing. She seemed to have no control over it, and she couldn't act on it. Not without making a fool of herself. Not without opening herself up to hurt.

A lose-lose situation if she'd ever seen one.

On a sigh, she rose. It was time to get on with her day. Now that the rolls were out of the oven, she could go for her run. The party of fishermen had left at the crack of dawn for an all-day excursion. The father and his sons were already loading up their boat and would be back in for rolls and juice an hour before they left for several days. If they followed tradition, the six women, who'd been coming to Crimson Falls for a week-long getaway for the past four years, wouldn't start wandering down to the dining room until after nine. Casey could handle them and just about anything else that came up in her absence.

"Is there anyplace to run around here?"

His question stopped her, both surprising and tickling her. It surprised her because she hadn't thought of him as a runner—although he did have the muscle tone. It tickled her because of the obvious.

"Gosh, let me think." She affected a puzzled scowl. "Where would a person who had access to fresh air and sunshine, and only about a thousand acres of wilderness area and forty miles of walking paths, run?"

His mouth twitched in a self-mocking semblance of a smile. "So sue me. I'm city-born and bred. If I don't see asphalt, I don't see possibilities."

She smiled. "Go get your running shoes on," she offered, against her better judgment. "I'll meet you at the dock and take you on the loop. What's your pleasure? A mile? Two miles?"

"Five's what I'm used to."

"Impressive," she said, surprised and pleased by his choice. "Five is what we'll do then. I'll see you in a couple of minutes."

He handed back the caramel roll. "Don't let this get away, okay? Me and my arteries will tackle it when we get back."

Smiling, she returned to the kitchen with the roll, and wrapped it up for him for later.

"How's he holding up?" Casey asked, as she filled a carafe with a mixture of white grape and orange juice to set out on the buffet table.

"He's chalked it up to bad wiring."

"Does that mean he's not moving?"

"Yes, sweet child who gets her kicks from Belinda badgering nonbelievers, that means he's not moving."

Casey's squeal of delight and, "Oh, goodie," had Scarlett shaking her head and grinning.

"How long do you think he'll last?"

Scarlett raised her brows. "I don't know. He's pretty determined. Couple more nights, maybe."

"What do you think she'll pull next? My money's on the bed."

"Nope," Scarlett said, considering. "It's supposed to rain tonight. I figure she'll opt for the window stunt."

"Quarter?" Casey suggested, with a challenging arch of her brow.

"You're on. And no IOUs this time," she admonished good-naturedly, as she headed for the back staircase and jogged up to the second floor to change. "I want the cold cash, child, or there'll be no more wagers for you."

Five

Clad in an NYU T-shirt and running shorts and shoes, Colin walked toward the dock to wait for Scarlett. Halfway there, he turned and looked back up at his bedroom window. He was still puzzled by what had happened last night. He was also determined to find an explanation. The bright light could have been a trick of moon glow and reflection from the lake. The shadows on the wall more of the same. As to the hot doorknob, there was undoubtedly a short somewhere in the wiring. The old brass hardware made an excellent conductor for electricity.

Even the sticking door—which he'd had a devil of a time getting open this morning—could be attributed to the aged and sagging state of the hotel. Everything was out of alignment. Later today he would hunt up a plane and shave some wood off the door to cure that problem.

He turned back to the lake and picked up his pace, confident in his conclusions. The dream, however, kept niggling away. It had been so vivid. So erotic. He could have sworn he'd dreamed in colors and scents and sensation—even though he never had before. The fact was, he rarely dreamed at all, or if he did he rarely remembered.

He remembered this one. The woman who'd come to him in the night had worn red. Something silk and sleek, falling off her shoulder, a long slit showing lots of leg. He could still feel the touch of her hands on his body. Still smell the lingering scent of her perfume that mingled with the fragrance of the flowers she'd carried.

She'd been exotic, alluring, wanton.

She'd been Scarlett Morgan, he admitted grudgingly as he reached the dock. And in his dreams she'd shared his bed, his body and his soul in a steamy night of passion.

"In your dreams is as far as it's going to get," he muttered, and started his stretching exercises. That was one conclusion he was sure of. Scarlett Morgan, with her red-gold curls and her sexy little body and wickedly gooey caramel rolls did not factor into any of his equations. The woman canned vegetables, for pity's sake. And made blueberry jam. She lacked both the sophistication and the callousness to enter into a casual affair and not feel diminished when it ended— which it would.

Now that he was past his initial surprise of finding her in this north-woods Club Med, he could get his libido under control. Just like he'd gotten over his initial irritation at being manipulated into coming here.

It had come to him on the dock last night that his friends may have been right. All work and no play made Colin a dull and horny boy. He'd been too long without the company of a woman. He could remedy that problem, once he returned to New York, to the mutual satisfaction of both himself and any number of partners—women who wanted the same thing out of the encounter as he did. Pleasure without pressure.

On that note of resolution, he was ready to run off some of his pent-up energy. Scarlett Morgan and his preoccupation with her, sexual or otherwise, was tucked tidily away on the shelf marked, Off Limits, Do Not Touch, until he turned and saw her walking toward him in her black shorts and running bra beneath a loose, pink tank top.

He propped his fists on his hips and hung his head. So much for hibernating libidos. No woman had a right to look that sexy and supple and desirable in running clothes. Her shoes were white and worn. Her socks were thick and pink and matched the shirt and the headband she'd slipped across her forehead. And that damn black spandex hugged every lush curve, every womanly ounce of flesh and bone and sleekly honed muscle.

"Ready to rock and roll?" she asked brightly as she adjusted her headband.

"Let's do it," he managed to say between clenched teeth, and fell into an easy jog beside her.

If he'd been familiar with the territory, he'd have picked up the pace and pulled away from her. Since that couldn't happen, his own exhaustion was his only hope. But as the first mile passed, and the path narrowed so that he had to run behind her, it became apparent that even if he ran ten miles, fatigue wasn't going to put a leash on his libido.

She stopped abruptly at a clearing. He was so intent on the unconsciously seductive movements of her hips that he almost ran her over.

"This is our old docking area." She pointed out a clearing that led to the lakeshore. "Up until this spring, our clients had to hike the mile to the hotel or wait for Geezer to come and pick them up in the Jeep. I'm hoping my money was well spent clearing out the shoreline and constructing the new dock closer to the hotel."

He just nodded, then fell into step behind her again when she resumed the run. The morning was cool, but the exertion quickly worked them both into a sweat. Her tank top clung to her skin as perspiration dampened the absorbent cotton. And though he tried to watch the path or the trees or the occasional glimpse of the lake that peeked through the forest when the running track neared the shoreline, his gaze was repeatedly drawn to her tidy little rear. She was compact, yet lean. Sleek, yet lush, an arresting combination of athlete and woman, maturity and youth.

He kept seeing her as he had last night—not in the bar, but in his dreams. In his bed. And suddenly five miles alone with her seemed like the Boston Marathon.

"How you doing back there?" she called over her shoulder.

"Fine," he muttered. "Just fine."

Amazingly, he made it though the run. She was marginally winded when they came full circle and jogged into a clearing that led them back to the dock.

"You're in pretty good shape for a city boy," she

said between labored breaths with a grin that acknowledged her approval.

"You're no slouch yourself. Obviously you do this on a regular basis," he said, with just a hint of hope that he was wrong. He didn't think he could take twelve more mornings of trailing her and not do something they'd both regret—like tackling her and taking her on the forest floor like an animal.

"I try to. Depends on how busy we are. Sometimes I can't work it in. Shouldn't be any problem this week."

That's what he was afraid of.

"Well..." She wiped the back of her wrist across her headband, "I'm going to hit the shower before I go back to work."

"I think I'll run another five." What he needed more than anything right now was to get away from her and the new image she'd just managed to create of her standing naked under a shower spray.

"Suit yourself. Do you think you can follow the right path and find your way back here?"

"If I can find my way around Manhattan, I think I can manage a few trees."

"Okay," she said warily, "but do stay aware of where you are. You can get lost in a flash in these woods."

"Yes, Mother," he replied cheekily, because he knew it would make her smile and because he had a sudden urge to see that smile again.

Fueled by it, he turned and headed back down the path. "Later." He waved over his shoulder and forced himself not to look back.

* * *

Much later he wasn't feeling so smart. Or so sure that running alone had been such a great idea.

"You're no Boy Scout, Slater," he grumbled aloud, when he walked by the same rock formation for the third time in the past hour. "You can't swim, you can't find your way out of the woods. If you had a blow torch, you probably couldn't start a fire, and you can bet your last stock dividends you couldn't tell a poison berry from a blueberry."

Aside from the embarrassment of getting lost, he was also getting hungry. At least he'd found something to take his mind off Scarlett's delectable little derriere. Her delicious caramel rolls shared top billing in his thoughts.

He stopped, looked up at the sunlight breaking through the trees and knew he ought to be able to figure out both the time and the direction by the sun's position.

It was times like these that he regretted certain aspects of his childhood. When other boys were joining Cub Scouts and youth groups and the "Y," he'd been hustling on the streets as a paperboy, or a stockboy or a gopher—all for the ultimate prize—money. It had always propelled him. It had always compelled him. It was the one thing his parents couldn't give him that he'd wanted.

He'd seen them struggle just to pay the bills. Seen them sacrifice their own pleasures so he and Cameron had food in their bellies and clothes on their backs. And he'd sworn at a very early age that he was going to make more money than his parents would ever know what to do with, then pay them back for the sacrifices they'd made.

It had taken him ten years, but he'd accomplished everything he'd set out to do. His parents lived in luxury between their Manhattan co-op and their beach house in the Keys. He'd taken his brother, Cameron, into the business as soon as he'd paid for his education, and he shared the wealth equally with him as a full partner.

Yes. He had everything he wanted. Everything but the ability to sit back and enjoy it. And a history of being a Boy Scout, he thought again grimly, and cursed the trees and his poor sense of direction.

He was debating whether or not he should turn around and head the other way when, from the corner of his eye, he caught a shadow of movement on the path ahead of him. He stopped cold as the shadow solidified—not into the shape of a bear, which he'd yet to see, but into one of a very large, very hungry-looking wolf.

A low, feral growl vibrated across the ten feet of pine-needle- and moss-covered forest floor separating them. Before he could fully assess the extent of the trouble he was in, another predator emerged from the dense foliage crowding the walking path. This one, though no less threatening, stood on two feet, not four.

He was a big man, well over six feet tall. Wearing a black T-shirt, worn denim jeans, moccasins and a leather headband that held back jet black hair reaching midway down his back, he quieted the wolf's threatening snarl with a slight motion of his hand.

Colin's immediate reaction to the sight of them, materializing out of thin air as if by magic, was that this place must actually be haunted. His second thought was much more rational, but no less daunting.

If they were as hostile as they looked, he was in big trouble.

Though he stood his ground, it didn't take a lengthy assessment to weigh his chances against the pair of them. Pitted against a wolf and this sullen man with the look of a warrior and an angry scar that ran from his temple to his jaw, there would be no contest. That didn't mean he wouldn't put up a good fight if it came down to it. He'd grown up on the streets of New York City. He may not have learned how to find his way out of a forest, but he'd learned a thing or two about self-defense.

"You would be Colin Slater?"

Still struggling with the man's intentions, and unsure if he and the wolf posed a physical threat, Colin was slow to answer.

"I would," he said warily.

The man moved gracefully toward him...at the last moment, extending his hand. "Whoa," he said, raising his palms in supplication. "I come in peace."

It was then that Colin realized he'd made fists of his hands and adopted a battle stance. Simultaneously it dawned on him that the slight tilting of the man's mouth, which would pass for a sneer on most men, was actually an amused grin.

"Abel Greene," he said in a tone that could arguably be considered friendly. "I'm a friend of Scarlett's. She sent me to look for you."

Slowly Colin relaxed his fists. Slower still, he extended his hand to return the gesture. Greene's handshake was firm but not overpowering. It was the last sign Colin needed.

"Sorry," he said, feeling sheepish. "I'm afraid the wolf spooked me."

Again came that almost smile. "Nashata has that effect on people, the first time they see her. She looks more wolf than dog when actually she's half of each."

"Nashata," Colin repeated, searching his memory, then coming up with scraps of a conversation with either Scarlett or Casey. "Then she would be the mother of Casey's puppies."

"So you've met the little hellions. J.D.'s chocolate Lab is the other responsible party."

He smiled, allowing the wolf-dog to sniff his hand. "It figures that Hazzard's dog would be as much of a rogue as his master." He met the big man's eyes, searching his memory once again. "Greene. Now I recognize the name. J.D.'s mentioned you. You and your wife live near his and Maggie's cabin, right? And sometimes help get Casey to school."

Greene nodded, and Colin got the distinct impression he was sizing him up. When the next words out of his mouth were "Scarlett's a good friend," which was a statement totally unrelated to their current situation, he knew he was right.

"She seems like a fine person," Colin said, feeling it judicious to avoid using the word *woman*, but not fully understanding why.

Greene considered him for a quite moment. "J.D. set you up, you know."

After his initial surprise at the accuracy of Greene's conclusion, Colin smiled, appreciating once again the candor of the people who populated Legend Lake. "We'd already figured that out."

"It's a nasty habit he has," Greene added. "In my case, though, you'll hear no complaints."

Colin wasn't sure how to react to that statement.

So he approached it carefully. "You met your wife because of J.D.?"

"Indirectly." That semblance of a smile whispered across his lips again. Just as quickly it was gone. "Are you ready to head back? Scarlett's a little worried that you'd gotten lost."

Colin saw no alternative but to bite the proverbial bullet. "It's hard to admit, but she's right. I *was* lost."

"No you weren't," Greene said amiably as he turned with the expectation that Colin would follow.

"I wasn't?" Colin fell in step behind them.

"Nope. You were just soaking up the scenery and were about to head back when Nashata found you. Anyway, that's the way I see it. But it'll be your story, so you can tell it any way you want to."

"I think I like your version," he conceded with a smile, and decided then and there that he liked this man. "Thanks," he added, buoyed by the prospect that he didn't have to lose face in front of Scarlett for the second time in as many days.

Until she saw Abel and Nashata walk out of the clearing with Colin in tow, Scarlett hadn't admitted to herself how worried she'd been. She stepped back from the dining room window and let go of a sigh of relief.

"So that's the way it is," her friend said.

She turned around and gave Abel's wife, Mackenzie, a blank look. "So that's the way *what* is?"

Mackenzie just grinned and, easing carefully up from the dining room table, walked to the window and peeked outside. "You were really concerned about him, weren't you?"

"Of course I was concerned," Scarlett said, working hard at not sounding defensive and giving herself away. "He's a guest. And whether I like it or not, a business partner. Naturally I was worried. I don't want anyone getting lost out there. It could be dangerous."

Mackenzie watched her husband and the guest in question walk toward the hotel. She turned back to Scarlett, a knowing look on her face. "He doesn't appear to me to be the kind of man who would have trouble taking care of himself. As a matter of fact, he looks capable of taking care of just about anything he sets his mind to. Tell me, Scarlett, has he set his mind on you?"

Scarlett was about to sputter out a laughing protest, when she recognized the look in her friend's sparkling green eyes. She tilted her head, considering. When comprehension dawned, she wagged an accusing finger Mackenzie's way. "You're in on this with J.D., aren't you?"

Mackenzie, petite and elflike, with her short, reddish hair and pixie nose, affected an expression of pure, perfected innocence. "I don't know what you're talking about."

Scarlett snorted. "And the lake isn't deep. J.D. sent you, didn't he? He's got it figured out that we're on to him by now, and instead of tossing his hat through the door to check out his welcome, he sent you to test the waters.

"Well, you can tell that hopelessly romantic meddler that his little ploy isn't working. I am *not* in the market for a man. Colin is *not* in the market for a woman. And furthermore, make sure he knows he ought to be ashamed of himself for sending a woman in your condition to do his dirty work."

Glowing, in the second trimester of her pregnancy, Mackenzie studied Scarlett for a moment, then shrugged. "Oh well. I tried." She walked back to the table and sat down. "But you've got to admit," she added, picking up where she'd left off on one of Scarlett's caramel rolls, "it wasn't such a bad idea. Colin Slater looks like hunk material to me."

Scarlett made a tsking sound. "This from a happily married and very pregnant woman."

"I'm married, not dead," Mackenzie said in her typical straightforward style. "And if I didn't have an eye for quality, I wouldn't be married to top-of-the-line material now."

In spite of her irritation, Scarlett smiled, remembering the unique circumstances under which Mackenzie and Abel had gotten together. In this day and age, the idea of a mail-order bride went against every feminist gene in her body, but she couldn't argue that it had turned into the perfect arrangement. She'd worried about the reclusive and brooding Abel for as long as she'd known him. The interruption of Mackenzie, and her fifteen-year-old brother, Mark, in Abel's isolated and solitary life had been the best kind of turmoil. And after a rough start, the match appeared to be perfect.

"I'll forgive you," she said, joining Mackenzie at the table. "Your hormones are haywire so you have an excuse. But J.D. had better walk softly and stay out of my path for a while, or I'll slice him up and use him for fish bait. Why does he think he knows what's best for me, anyway? And how dare he presume to arrange my relationships."

Mackenzie chewed thoughtfully on a bite of roll. "Maybe he figures that since he was responsible for talking Abel into advertising for a wife and it worked out for us that he has a knack for matchmaking.''

"He has a knack for interfering, nothing more," Scarlett amended, as she rose to get more hot water for Mackenzie's herbal tea.

"So what you're saying is that you don't find Colin Slater attractive," Mackenzie said, noting how fidgety Scarlett was.

"I didn't say that," Scarlett corrected. "I'm not dead, either." They shared a grin. "But I'm not shopping for a man. And if I was, Colin Slater wouldn't be on the list. For heaven's sake, we have nothing in common. He's a New Yorker. He eats, breaths and sleeps business. He's about as comfortable in the north woods as I am in the city. And I'm as far from being his type of woman as…''

When she trailed off, unable to come up with an adequate comparison, Mackenzie supplied one for her. "As different as I am from Abel?" she asked brightly.

Scarlett frowned. "That's different."

"How is it different?"

"It just is," she said irritably. "Look, I don't even know why we're talking about this."

After gracing her with an irritatingly smug grin, Mackenzie took another sip of her tea.

"It's not going to happen," Scarlett insisted. "So you can just get that 'we'll see' look out of your eyes."

"Hmm" was all Mackenzie said.

With a shake of her head, Scarlett muttered her frustration, then jerked her head around when she heard the sound of the men approaching the dining room.

"It looks fine," Mackenzie whispered, and only then did Scarlett realize she'd touched a hand to her hair to smooth it.

"I wasn't doing it for him," she snapped, then jumped at the sound of Abel's voice.

"You weren't doing what for who?" he asked as he and Colin joined them at the table.

"Geezer," she improvised quickly. "I...I wasn't cleaning the bar this morning for him. It's...it's not a job I expect him to do." She shot a quick, fidgety look Colin's way, then felt herself flush all over at his open and thorough study of her face.

Abel pulled out a chair beside Mackenzie and, seemingly oblivious to the undercurrents of awareness humming around the table, sat down. "Feeling okay?" he asked in that intimate, protective voice Scarlett had learned to recognize as the one he reserved only for his wife.

"I'm great. Scarlett has fed me, pampered me and coddled me like a mother hen."

"My wife, Mackenzie," Abel said, turning from her to Colin. "Mackenzie, this is Colin Slater. He was just on his way back when Nashata and I ran into him."

"Nice to meet you, Mackenzie." Colin extended his hand across the table.

"My pleasure." Mackenzie returned his smile. "I hope you're finding your stay at Crimson Falls and Legend Lake to your liking."

Colin's mouth twisted into a semblance of a grin. "It's...certainly different from what I'm used to."

"Different good, I hope," she persisted.

He thought a moment then conceded with a slight nod. "Yeah, I guess you could say that. The country's beautiful. The falls are spectacular. It's the quiet that's giving me trouble."

"It'll grow on you," Mackenzie assured him. "Trust me. I was born and raised in L.A., so I know what you're talking about. It was a little unsettling for me at first, too, but now nothing could compel me to go back."

"Mr. Slater will have to take your word on that," Scarlett interjected, rising from the table. "He's only here for a couple of weeks and then it's back to New York."

Mackenzie's eyes danced between Scarlett and Colin. "Well, that's unfortunate. But isn't it nice to know Crimson Falls and Scarlett's good cooking are only a few hours away by plane?"

Scarlett felt her color rise again. She sent a warning look Mackenzie's way before turning to Colin. "Are you ready for that caramel roll now?"

"Thought you'd never ask." He gave her a probing look. "I should shower first but I've been thinking about that roll for the past hour."

"Coming right up," she said in her best, breezy, innkeeper's voice and made a beeline for the kitchen.

They were all still sitting around the table, looking relaxed and comfortable with each other when she returned. Not fair, she thought. Not fair at all, considering her heart was still skipping and slipping at the thought of Colin's eyes and the way he'd looked at her when he'd first come into the room. Like she was dessert and he had a sweet tooth.

"Where's Mark?" Abel asked as he scooted his chair closer to Mackenzie to make more room for Scarlett.

"He and Casey are out back playing with the puppies."

"How's Mark doing?" Scarlett asked, still achingly aware of Colin's gaze on her as he pulled out a chair for her so she could sit down beside him.

"Mark is amazing." Mackenzie's smile was full of pride and love. "Since I got him out of the city and, with Abel's help, got him settled in here, he's a different boy."

Scarlett was glad. She was well aware of Mark's troubled past as a gang member in the streets of L.A. It was Mackenzie's desperation to get him out of the web of danger and crime that had ultimately led her to answer Abel's ad. Their story was one of those fantastic, unbelievable tales that gave her faith in the goodness of the human condition and the healing power of love.

At least it worked for some people, she conceded, watching Mackenzie and Abel together. It had also worked for J.D. and Maggie. Maggie had been severely wounded by a damaging relationship when she'd escaped to Legend Lake and Blue Heron Bay a year ago. J.D. had found her there and cured her with his love.

And now he was determined to wrap up Scarlett's love life in a neat and tidy package with pretty ribbons and bows. She had a news flash for him. Colin Slater was not about to be wrapped up by anyone. And even if he was, she would "return to sender" unopened.

She made a concentrated effort to avoid looking at him as he sat beside her. It was difficult. She'd been supercharged with awareness since this morning. First, when he'd been running beside her, she'd been far too cognizant of the strength of his muscular thighs, the breadth of his chest as he regulated his breathing to match his long strides, the sheen of perspiration, slick on his skin as he'd worked up a sweat. When the path had narrowed and he'd fallen into step behind her, her heartbeat had accelerated—not so much from the exertion of the run, but from the knowledge that his gaze was tracking every move she made. Five miles had never seemed so long.

And the past hour had seemed like ten as she'd worried and wondered if he was lost out there. The thought of anything happening to him had made something inside twist and ache...too much. Just like the thought of him leaving in twelve days hurt too much. Way too much, since she'd only just met him. Way too much, considering there could never be a future for them under any circumstances.

Six

"So everything's going okay for you over here?" Scarlett heard Abel ask through the tangled maze of her thoughts.

"Great." She forced a smile and made herself concentrate on something other than her futile feelings for Colin Slater. "And thanks to the raffle, I've got enough of a nest egg to start on some more of those repairs."

"I don't have to remind you that I want to help you, right?"

"You've already helped. Abel built my new dock," she explained to Colin. "He's a master contractor. Besides building his own log cabin, he custom designs and constructs them as a business.

"And no, you don't have to remind me," she said for Abel's benefit, then, to keep the conversation flowing she mentioned that Colin was also in construction.

"More or less," he clarified. "Unlike Abel, we don't start from the ground up. We're more into renovation and restoration."

"That's perfect," Mackenzie said brightly. "Scarlett needs all the help she can get restoring the hotel."

It took everything in her to keep from glaring at Mackenzie. The woman could give meddling lessons to J.D.

"Colin isn't helping with the renovation," she informed them quickly. "He's here for a vacation."

"And the fact is, I haven't been asked to help," Colin added with a look that Scarlett had difficulty translating.

Colin was having a little trouble sorting out what he meant, too. When he'd arrived yesterday, he'd had no intention of getting embroiled in Scarlett's problems with the hotel's renovations. Now here he was, only a day later, and the more he saw of her day-to-day struggle, the more he realized he wanted to help out. And then there was the fact that if he didn't find something to do with his hands soon, he couldn't guarantee that he wouldn't keep them off the hotel's owner. Volunteering his services suddenly seemed like the wisest thing to do.

"I think you've just had another offer," Mackenzie said, correctly interpreting his statement. "It wouldn't be polite to turn it down."

"It wouldn't be polite to impose on a guest," Scarlett said, looking, in Colin's opinion, just a little bit harried.

"She's not imposing, is she, Colin?" Mackenzie persisted, ignoring the warning look Scarlett shot her way. "I'll bet you're just itching to dig into any number of projects around here."

Colin grinned. Mackenzie Greene, it seemed, was as determined as her cohort, J. D. Hazzard to start something between him and Scarlett.

Since he was just as determined to keep his distance, and despite the increasing difficulty in doing so, he decided to humor her and do something for Scarlett at the same time. Hopefully the side benefit would be that it would save him from idle time and idle thoughts…like how good this roll would taste if he was licking the caramel from Scarlett's skin instead of from a stainless steel fork.

"Now that you mention it," he said, "I was considering asking Scarlett if she'd mind if I did a little work for her."

"Mind? She wouldn't mind. She'd be relieved that someone was taking some of the burden of this place off her shoulders."

"I don't consider Crimson Falls a burden," Scarlett said between tightly clenched teeth.

"Of course you don't," Mackenzie amended quickly. "I meant that with all of the other things you have to do around here to keep you busy, an extra pair of hands would be appreciated."

"I think maybe it's time we got you back home," Abel said with an indulgent look at his wife, before turning an apologetic but amused gaze on Scarlett. "She's wound up like a thunderbird in an electrical storm, and sometimes she doesn't know to quit while she's ahead."

"You have to leave so soon?"

Colin noted that while Scarlett's protest sounded sincere, her relief was also evident. Mackenzie's not-

so-subtle attempts to throw them together and to paint Scarlett as a woman in need of a man around the house had rattled her big-time.

"We have to leave," Abel stated firmly, and helped his marginally miffed wife to her feet. "I want to make the crossing before the winds rise and the lake gets choppy. A storm front's moving in tonight, and we can't be subjecting you or the baby to any rough water."

Mackenzie smiled lovingly at Abel, then turned to Scarlett with an elaborate sigh. "I love it when he gets all husbandly."

Abel snorted. "I sincerely hope this child does not come equipped with your smart mouth."

"You love it," she returned cheekily, and Colin could see by the look on Abel's face that he did.

Feeling as though he was intruding on a private moment, he looked away. Without conscious thought, his gaze went straight to Scarlett's. She, too, had averted her attention from the tender looks passing between husband and wife, and he sensed what she was feeling. It was the same thing he was feeling. A sense of loss. Acute, cutting loss—for everything Abel and Mackenzie shared. For everything that Scarlett had never had and deserved. For his own inability to commit to anything beyond the scope of his business. And suddenly he was struck by a deep feeling of regret.

He was stunned. He understood why a woman like Scarlett would have feelings of something missing. He had no understanding of why he was struggling with them. He was perfectly content with his life the way it was. He didn't need an intimate relationship—

emotional or physical—to feel complete. And yet here he sat, numbed by the emptiness that gripped him.

Scarlett met his eyes, then quickly glanced away. "I'll go get Mark."

In silence, he watched her walk out of the room.

"She's a very special person." Mackenzie's tone was soft, her eyes searching.

Colin drew a deep breath before addressing Mackenzie with a quick, thoughtful smile. "Yes. She is."

"Pretty, too."

Abel shook his head, gently gripped his wife's arm and led her toward the door.

"Enough, woman." He sent Colin another apologetic look over Mackenzie's head.

Yeah. Enough, Colin thought. Enough of this introspective conjecturing about what his life would be like with someone like Scarlett to share it.

The night was dark and overcast. The wind Abel had expressed concern about had picked up. Colin stood on the end of the dock, his hands shoved deep in his pockets. Oblivious to the night chill and the gusts that whipped the bay into rolling, white-capped swells, he thought back to the events of the day.

After meeting Mackenzie's younger brother Mark, he'd bid his goodbyes and taken a quick shower. Then, looking for something to occupy his time, he'd double-checked with Scarlett to make sure she really didn't mind if he tinkered around.

"I want to start with the door to my room," he'd explained. Graciously, but with reservations that she'd tried to hide, she'd assured him that if that was the way he wanted to spend his vacation, he was welcome to do anything he wanted.

Anything he wanted. If she only knew.

With a weary shake of his head, he resumed his distracted study of the night.

He'd planed the door to his room until he was certain there was no way it could stick again. He'd repaired the porch board he'd nearly tripped over yesterday. He'd waited until she'd left the kitchen after lunch, then replaced the washers in the dripping faucet.

It was while he was standing on the verandah, contemplating what other Band-Aid fixes he could perform on a structure that needed major surgery, that the women had approached him. Shyly at first, but then with a flirtatious friendliness he'd found hard to resist, they'd roped him into a game of cards. They delighted in teaching him hearts, promising him with teasing smiles that they'd work up to strip poker if he'd rather play that particular game.

They'd been outrageous, and absolutely harmless, he'd realized. As the afternoon had worn on, he'd let them lure him into a state of relaxation he hadn't imagined he'd had in him to feel. When they'd conned him into playing pool in the bar and then proceeded to beat the pants off him, he'd called it quits. They'd good-naturedly offered him a rematch anytime he wanted one and then had headed to the dock to soak up some sun. With that distraction gone, he'd hunted down Geezer and helped him mow the lawn.

Even now, as he stood on the dock and thought back, he'd known what he'd been doing. He'd been running. And hiding. From emotions that felt raw and exposed. From the unsolicited sensations Scarlett Morgan stirred up every time their gazes accidentally collided.

She had neither the sophistication nor the guile to hide the confusion she was feeling. He both damned and treasured that lack of calculation. Those liquid, telling eyes of hers gave away every emotion. She wanted him. She was afraid of wanting him. She knew it wasn't wise to want him.

Just like he wanted her. Was afraid of wanting her. Knew it wasn't wise to want her.

He lifted his face to the wind and sincerely hoped she had the strength to cling to her convictions, because he sure as hell was having trouble sticking to his.

"I don't have to worry about you falling asleep standing up, do I?"

He'd been so preoccupied thinking about Scarlett, he hadn't heard her step onto the dock. Only when he turned and felt a rich flood of pleasure wash through him, did he realize that no matter how much he told himself it was wrong, he'd been hoping she would come looking for him.

He smiled in the dark. "I don't think there's much danger of that."

But there was danger here. Danger in the way his heart thundered as she approached...tentatively, with her hands tucked in the pockets of a light weight jacket, her tanned bare legs looking even darker in the night.

He bit back a rueful smile, wondering when he'd strayed so far away from the convictions that had ruled his life. Business had always been first. Then he'd met Scarlett Morgan, and all she had to do was stand there and he was lost in the wanting for something more.

She was beguiling in the dark, enticing beneath the

heavy sky and beside the restless water. The wind played with the fine curling wisps of her hair. The night shadowed and shaded the delicate contours of her face, nearly hiding the vulnerability in her eyes.

"We worked you pretty hard today," she said, tipping her face into the wind, intentionally avoiding eye contact.

Obviously he hadn't worked hard enough or he'd be in bed now. Asleep. Alone. Instead of contemplating that bed with both of them in it.

"It felt good to be doing something with my hands," he said, trying to put some distance between them with conversation—no matter how inane. "Before Slater Corporation got so big, we were still working on brownstones and apartment buildings. I used to do a lot of the actual renovation work myself. I don't get a chance to dig in much anymore. Too much paperwork. Too much travel. I realized today how much I've missed it."

"Well," her tension was evident in her continued reluctance to look at him. "I hope you didn't let Geezer take advantage of you."

He smiled in spite of himself. "I don't let anyone take advantage unless I want to be taken advantage of."

"Like the way the girls did this afternoon?"

He chuckled, remembering. "They're quite the crew. I don't think I've ever been around women who had so much fun just entertaining each other. They laughed constantly."

He studied her soft smile in profile and knew he wanted to see it a hundred other ways. Looking up at him from his pillow. Looking down at him in the throes of passion.

"I always enjoy the week they spend here—the way they let loose. They make me feel like a kid again."

The wistfulness in her voice shifted his thoughts from desire to anger—not at her but for her. "A kid who works all the time and watches from a distance, while everyone else has fun?"

When she just shrugged, he pressed her. "What does Scarlett Morgan do for fun, anyway? Besides work in her garden and take care of everyone else?"

Again she lifted a shoulder, then wrapped her jacket tighter against the buffet of the wind. "When I have time, I read. I listen to music. Sometimes I get around to watching one of the movies J.D. is always lending me from his collection of classics."

"That's it?"

She squared her shoulders defensively. "That's it. And it's enough. But what about you?" she countered, finally turning to face him. "From the account J.D. gave me, all you do is work. What do you do for fun in *your* life?"

Nothing, he admitted to himself reluctantly. He didn't know when regret for that omission had settled in. He suspected, though, that it was his lack of attention to more frivolous needs that had him in this fix right now. This fix of wanting something more—to distraction. Something, or someone.

"Point taken," he conceded. "So we're both guilty of working too hard. Old habits are hard to break, I guess."

The longing in his voice must have alerted her. Just as the understanding in her eyes had him moving toward her.

"Maybe the question now," he said, searching her

face for a warning to back away, "is what are we going to do about it?"

Even before he asked, he knew the thrust of their conversation had shifted. Even as she stood there, her eyes alight with hesitancy and a shimmering, forbidden excitement, he sensed she knew it, too.

They weren't talking about their work habits. They weren't talking about leisure activities. He wasn't sure they ever had been. That idle bit of chatter had been filler, a temporary diversion to keep them from dealing with the real issue of why he was standing here on the dock and why she had sought him out.

"What are we going to do about what?"

Her voice had dropped to a soft, tentative whisper. No competition for the pummeling wind and the crash of water on the shore, but he heard her, anyway, and he knew the issue as surely as she did.

It was inevitable. Had been destined to happen since he'd first seen her in her kitchen with frosting on her cheek and surprise in her eyes. He'd wanted her then with a stunning certainty. He wanted her now with a ruthless urgency.

"What are we going to do about this," he murmured, gave in to the need and lowered his mouth toward hers.

Scarlett knew she shouldn't let it happen. She knew she shouldn't just stand there as he moved toward her. His intent was as clear as lake water by sunlight. But she couldn't move, couldn't breathe, as he searched her face beneath the cloud-covered sky.

He was going to kiss her. And she was going to like it. And want it. And want him in ways she'd never wanted another man.

The hands that gripped her shoulders were strong

but not possessive; his body next to hers, a warm and welcome buffer against the wind. In his eyes was a hunger, reckless and dark that mingled with apology for what he was about to do.

She lost it all then. Her resolution. Her ability to deny him. She forgot about wisdom and mistakes and consequences and raised a trembling hand to his face.

With the wind sighing around them and the water washing up over the dock, she let him draw her against his taut, hard body and into his kiss as effortlessly as dusk drawing darkness from light.

It was everything his eyes had promised. He was all she'd imagined—neither tentative, nor apologetic as he touched his mouth to hers. He didn't ask but neither did he dominate as his touch transcended to something deeper and darker and infinitely more consuming.

His mouth was hard and demanding. Yet he offered and took with equal measure, enticing her to a flash point of pure physical need. This was passion as she'd never experienced it. This was pleasure like she'd never known. And it was something she'd lived without for far too long.

His scent surrounded her, masculine and woodsy, laced with the lake wind, heated by his arousal. The taste of him, strong coffee and after-dinner wine and a hunger she hadn't imagined she could foster, was a tangible enticement too delicious to deny. When he drew her tighter in his arms and groaned his pleasure into her mouth, she melted against him like chocolate beneath a beating sun.

She wanted it to go on forever. The kiss. The contact. The feelings he'd awakened that were rich and heady and real. But forever was for fairy tales, and that's something her life had never been.

She didn't stop him; yet slowly, with a lingering resistance and a necessary resolve, he raised his head. His hand was shaking when he touched it to her hair. His breath was ragged as he folded her against him and pressed her face into the hollow of his throat. She felt his pulse beating there and knew he was as aroused as she was—and just as reluctant to end it.

And possibly, he was just as confused.

"Scarlett..."

Her name on his lips was little more than a whisper, but she heard so much in that one, raspy word. Regret. Need. Resolution.

She drew in and let out a deep breath. "I know."

She made herself move out of the circle of his arms. Turning toward the lake, she crossed her arms over her waist to stall the chill the wind and his absence created. "Big mistake, that."

Soundlessly he moved behind her. After a moment's hesitation, he tugged her back against his chest. He let out a deep breath and rested his chin on the top of her head. "You regret it?"

She covered the arms he'd folded around her with her hands. "I didn't say that. I said it was a mistake."

His silence confirmed his agreement. "So," he said finally, his warm breath feathering through her hair, "what are we going to do about it?"

With a lethargy she had no business feeling, she smiled. "I believe that was the question that got us into this."

Again a prolonged silence passed before he ended it. "And what, exactly, are we into here?"

While he attempted to make the question light, his tone relayed his unease.

She knew she should move away from him. But the warmth and strength of his chest against her back felt too good and too right for something that was so wrong. She stayed where she was, promising herself it was only for a few minutes more. She hadn't known how much she'd missed being held by a man. Hadn't known how much she'd missed the sensual side of being a woman.

"I think the term is deep water," she said finally.

"Yeah," he agreed, sounding weary. "I think maybe it is."

For several oddly comforting minutes they stood together, she, leaning back against him, he, holding her close from behind. Both of them wondering how they were going to back away from this, when their heads were at odds with their hearts.

"I'm not up for a casual affair, Colin." She hated the tremor in her voice and the artlessness of her admission. Still, she stayed the course. "And we both know that's all this could ever be."

His arms tightened before he exhaled a deep breath, then slowly let her go. "I know. And I'm sorry. I wish it could be otherwise."

She turned to him. Even in the darkness she could see his regret, see the lingering heat of his desire. But most of all she saw the man who had made her feel alive, as a woman, for the first time since the death of her marriage. For that gift she would always be grateful. "You've nothing to be sorry for."

Colin searched her face as she stood there. She looked vulnerable and vital and determined, all at the same time. He couldn't remember ever wanting a woman more—or when he'd made a mistake as big as pulling her into his arms.

She wasn't having any of his regrets, though. But neither was she going to let this go further. With a soft smile she assured him that all was well. Then, exercising a wisdom he'd do well to imitate, she bid him good-night and walked away.

"You're so wrong," he whispered, too low for her to hear. He did have something to be sorry for. For the first time in his life, he was truly sorry he couldn't offer a woman—that he couldn't offer *this* woman— what she needed from him as a man.

"Now, I could understand why a person would wanna run if he had someplace t' go," Geezer grumped, as he thumbed back his cap and satisfied an itch on the top of his bald head. "But t' just run around in a circle in the woods like a bear chasin' his tail, it don't make no sense."

Colin listened to Geezer's grousing with half an ear, as he walked a slow circle to cool down and regain his breath. He'd done a brisk five miles at day-break. Another five as a bonus, or penance, he couldn't decide which. He'd just known he had to get out of that hotel and away from its women and its quirks before he drew some conclusions he'd been trying to avoid. And he didn't want to chance running into Scarlett on the trail.

"So, what'd Belinda pull last night? Shakin' bed or open window?" Geezer asked without preamble. "The little girl and her momma got a bet on it, and I'm holding the quarters."

Colin sent the old man a suspicious look. "What do you know about what happens in that room?"

Geezer snorted. "I know three night's the record for a man t' stay there and you're pushing it."

"You're not going to tell me you buy into that spirit-of-a-soiled-dove nonsense."

"Me? I don't have t' believe it. I'm not sleeping in there. I'm only holding the money. So what was it?" he persisted, as he hobbled over to the dock to untie the bow line on a boat for the party of departing fishermen.

Colin moved to help him. Squatting on his haunches, he reached for the slip knot and tugged it free, just as the last man clambered into the boat with a bucketful of bait.

"Don't catch 'em all," Geezer grumbled over the roar of the outboard motor as they pulled away. "Just more work for me when they bring 'em in," he sputtered, then ambled back to his deck chair in the shade of the boat house.

Once he was comfortable, he closed his eyes and tugged his hat down low. "Shakin' bed or open window?" he asked again.

"The window," Colin admitted. Staring out over the lake, he dragged a hand through his hair. "But there's a perfectly logical explanation."

"Humph."

"Those windows are ancient. Double hung. Strung with old rope and weights and pulleys," he insisted, walking through all the possibilities as he spoke. He'd already played this game with himself—several times—just like he had during the night when he'd wakened repeatedly to find rain beating in the very window he'd shut an hour earlier. He'd felt like a Ping-Pong ball, he'd bounced in and out of bed so many times. "Something's out of alignment."

"Just like something's out of alignment with the door t' Belinda's room?"

Colin scowled. He'd had trouble getting it open again this morning. "The rain made the wood swell. I'll plane it again today."

"Got an answer for everything, don'tcha?"

"All it takes is a little deductive reasoning."

"Same kind you used when you put the moves on that little lady last night?"

Colin glared at him.

"I can't help what I seen. I was awake. My gout was fired up. So I was pacing it out. Good thing, too." He slanted Colin a look that said he was lower than the lake bottom, in Geezer's book. "I knew you was slippery."

"What happened last night between Scarlett and me is none of your business."

"You don't listen so good, boy. I warned you, first off, that she is my business and you're not t' do anything t' cause her hurt."

"And I told you, first off, that it is not my intention to hurt her."

"Then keep yer distance."

"Look, not that I owe you an explanation, but I didn't plan to kiss her. And I don't plan on a repeat. We both know it would be a mistake, all right? We've both got our own agendas, and they aren't compatible."

Geezer snorted. "I don't know nothing about no fancy words like *agendas* and *compatible*, but I know the way she looks at you, and it looks like heartbreak t' me."

Geezer's assessment fostered a guilt Colin had been

trying to avoid. To combat it, he glared at the old man. "What are you to her, anyway?"

Geezer pursed his lips, then laced his fingers across his middle. "It ain't so much what I am t' her as what she is t' me." The affection in his voice relayed the depth of his feelings for Scarlett. "She give me a job when everybody else told me I was used up. She took me in when I had no place t' go. And she loves this lake like I do, and she wants t' keep it the way it is.

"What she is t' me is a fine woman and my friend. If she was my own daughter, I couldn't care about her more."

Colin considered him for a long moment. "I'd say she's a lucky woman to have such loyalty." He drew in and let out a frustrated breath. "I don't want to hurt her, Geezer. I just want to get through the next week and a half and then get back to my business."

Geezer eyed him critically, then averted his gaze to the lake. "So stick t' the plan. But as long as you're here, it wouldn't hurt you none t' help her out a bit."

Colin nodded. "Hard as it might be for you to believe, that's one more thing we agree on."

"Then get to it, boy." He tugged his cap over his eyes and settled in for a mid-morning nap. "Time's a wastin'."

Seven

The next morning Colin's day started out with the door to his room—again. If he accomplished nothing else in the next week, that damn door was not going to stick, although he'd be damned if he could figure out why it never presented a problem when he went *into* the room. It was just when he wanted to get out that it gave him trouble.

For the next two days and nights he did everything he could, short of rudeness, to avoid Scarlett. He made brief appearances at breakfast, then he'd haul out the tool chest and go to work. He started on the windows—specifically the one in his room. Every day, he'd work until lunch, slip into the dining room, eat a quick bite, then work the rest of the afternoon. He'd repeat another eat-and-run at dinnertime and then make himself scarce—even from Casey, who'd gotten into the habit of tagging along and was wheedling her way into his heart despite his resolve not to let her. At night, after a trip to the dock that was beginning to feel like a ritual, he'd turn in and tell himself there was nothing strange going on in his room.

Except that there was.

One night he'd awakened several times with the odd sensation that the bed was shaking. The moment he'd wakened, whatever it was that had roused him had stopped. It was only in the morning, after being repeatedly jerked out of sleep by a vibrating sensation, that he'd accepted the fact that the bed had moved a good three feet toward the middle of the room.

"The floor in that room slopes downward," he'd told Geezer, when he'd pressed him about his nights in Belinda's room. "For that matter, there's not a level floor in the whole place. And the hotel does a little more settling every day."

Geezer had just harrumphed his usual cynic's response, sat back and asked Colin how many times he'd planed the door.

The next couple of nights were relatively uneventful—unless he considered that like every night since he'd been there, his dreams had been vivid, colorful and arousing. While he'd been relatively successful in keeping away from Scarlett between dawn and dusk, his nights were filled with her. Her taste. Her scent. The promise of her fierce and sultry passion.

He woke up one morning to fire searing through his blood—and a room so cold he expected to see frost on the windowpanes. He threw back the covers, walked shivering to the window and opened it. The warmth of the July morning rolled in through the window, sweet, cleansing, fresh. He stood there for a long moment, his face to the sun, an arctic chill at his back, and told himself it was all in his imagination—like a subconscious cold shower to help cool the effects of his erotic dream.

He got the hell out of there, just the same. He tugged on his running clothes, fought with the door until he swore, and finally managed to jerk it open. He didn't look back; he didn't think about the room or about Scarlett. He just ran. And ran until he slumped against a tree in exhaustion. And then he went through the rest of the day the way he planned to go through every remaining one until his two weeks were up: with a single-minded determination to keep his distance.

Only, his plans, like his resolve, were destined to be broken.

It was the day Scarlett had been dreading. The hotel was empty. The party of fisherman had limited out, packed their catch in dry ice and headed for home. The women had maxed out on their vacation time and had reluctantly bid her goodbye until next year. The man and his sons weren't due back from the boundary waters until the day after tomorrow, and her next bookings weren't due to arrive for two days. Even Geezer, taking advantage of the short break in the action, had decided that he couldn't put off a visit to his sister in Bordertown any longer.

And then there was Casey. She deserved some time away from the hotel. When Mackenzie had contacted Scarlett on the shortwave radio and asked if Casey could spend the weekend with them, Scarlett's immediate response had been yes. She couldn't deny her daughter this chance to have some fun with the Greenes.

Mark arrived early, just a little past eight. He took the time to wolf down a couple of caramel rolls, then helped load Casey and the pups into the boat.

"Did you remember to pick up the basket of goodies I made for you to take along? There's a casserole for dinner and some fresh bread and enough rolls for breakfast for a couple of mornings."

"Don't worry, Ms. Morgan. I'd forget Casey before I'd forget to pack your rolls," Mark assured her with a grin and an exaggerated "ouch!" when Casey playfully punched him in the arm.

She couldn't help but smile at Mark's teasing. Mackenzie was right. He'd come a long way from the sullen and surly and very troubled kid Mackenzie had dragged there from California last December.

"How many times have I asked you to call me Scarlett?" she prompted good-naturedly. "This 'Ms. Morgan' business makes me feel old."

"Sorry, Ms. M— I mean, Scarlett."

"Much better. You two have a good time, and, Casey, I'll see you in a couple of days, sweetie."

She stood on the dock, watched the boat diminish to a silver speck in the midst of blue water and fought the significance of Casey's departure. Casey had been her last wall of defense. She was now alone with the one man she couldn't afford to be alone with.

Turning slowly, she looked toward the hotel, drew a bracing breath and told herself to shape up.

"You have nothing to worry about," she assured herself. Since that night on the dock when he'd kissed her, Colin had kept his distance so well that the Grand Canyon could have been between them. She'd only caught glimpses of him—as he'd finished his run, as she'd walked down the hall and found him determinedly planing the door to his room, as he'd grabbed a quick bite, then disappeared.

If he could do it, so could she. All she had to do was keep her own distance and it should work out just fine.

With the determination that had gotten her into her sixth season at Crimson Falls, she pushed back her sleeves and set out to do a little recreational gardening and, unfortunately, a lot of wondering. What would it be like, making love with Colin Slater?

She got rained out at noon. The clouds moved in quickly. So quickly she got soaked in the downpour. Gathering the armload of snapdragons she'd cut for centerpieces, she sprinted to the kitchen door and ducked inside.

After dumping the flowers in the sink, to deal with them later, she scooted from window to window, shutting them against the rain. That done, she ran up the back stairs to the second floor and closed the windows in her quarters. Only then did she strip off her soggy clothes and step into the shower.

The last she'd seen of Colin had been a glimpse of him going into the boat house down by the dock. Grateful that the rain had caught him there, instead of in the hotel with her, she toweled her hair dry. Not bothering to run a brush through it, she slipped into her robe and, barefoot, walked back downstairs to the kitchen.

The clouds, plump and black and swollen with rain they had yet to shed, scudded across the afternoon sky, darkening the day to gray, twilight hues. Thunder rolled across the lake land. It was the kind of afternoon that cried out for a good book, a cup of hot tea and a comfortable chair to curl up in. Wishing she could indulge herself in that very lazy activity, Scarlett put the flowers in water to keep them fresh and set the teakettle on a burner to boil.

A few minutes later, with her cup of tea in one hand and a small vase full of snapdragons in the other, she ambled back upstairs to settle in to some much-neglected bookwork.

Just as she reached the top step, lightning flashed like a strobe. Thunder clamored in its wake, rumbling like a squadron of kettle drums, shaking the windows and rattling the doors.

She walked down the hall to her room and was about to burrow in for the duration, when she realized she hadn't checked the window in Belinda's room.

Setting her tea on a hall table and, on a whim, deciding to leave the vase of flowers for Colin, she approached his closed door.

He'd been in the boat house glazing windows when he'd noticed the clouds roll in. He'd almost made it to the verandah when the first big downburst let fly. By the time it was raining in earnest, he was inside, the door shut soundly behind him.

The empty hotel spelled trouble. Avoiding Scarlett would be damn near impossible now. It had been hard enough with people around as a buffer. With nothing but the walls and his good intentions between them, his restraint would be stretched to the limit.

The safest place at the moment appeared to be his room. He decided to wait out the storm there until it passed and he could go back about his business. By himself. Away from Scarlett. Safe. Sane. Solitary.

Shrugging out of his wet shirt, he toed off his shoes and, wearing only his slacks, lay back on the bed. Lacing his hands behind his head, he stared at the ceiling and listened to the rain pepper the windows. And the sound of the back door slamming shut. Of Scarlett hurrying through the first floor closing windows. Of her muffled footsteps on the back stairs, the distant hiss of her shower and the complaint of ancient water pipes.

He closed his eyes to block the picture of her in the shower, the water sluicing over her bare skin, her face tipped to the steamy spray, her hands running the length of her body, soapy, slippery...

With a groan, he tried to concentrate on the storm. The only thunder he heard was that of his rampaging heart. He wasn't sure how much time had passed, when he heard soft footsteps approach his door.

As still as stone he lay there. As silent as midnight, he waited. Slowly the brass knob turned. Slower still, the door eased open. Telling himself he was dreaming, hoping against hope he wasn't, he turned his head toward the door.

She was standing there—the woman who had haunted his nights.

Just as in his dreams, she wore a red silk robe, softly slipping off one shoulder, slightly parted to reveal a length of long, tanned leg. Her hair was wet, her eyes were huge, the flowers she carried as fragrant as the flesh beneath all that sultry silk.

"I-I'm sorry. I...I thought you were in the boat house. I...I was just going to check your window and...and leave these for you."

He raised up on an elbow, unable to take his eyes off her as she waited there, hesitant, vulnerable, and as beautiful as she was every night when she came to him in his sleep.

"I-I'll just—I'll just set them on the table... over... there."

Her eyes asked for permission, relayed her awareness... of the intimacy implicit as she stood in his room in only her robe, of him lying half-dressed on the bed, of the magic a man and a woman could make in each others arms.

Silk shifted over her lush curves as she crossed the room and, with trembling hands, set the flowers on the table by the window. For a long moment she stood there. Her back to him. Her head down. Her hands clasped around the vase as if it was her anchor and she was adrift in a sea of uncertainty. Her shadow dancing across the faded wallpaper in the darkening afternoon.

Wind, rain and thunder clashed outside the window. The battle of elements was nothing compared to the war he waged within himself to keep from asking her to stay.

Everything about her was captivating: the slender curve of her hip, the sheen of her hair, tumbling in wild, damp curls about her face. And when she turned slowly away from the window, her lashes lowered, her breath rapid and shallow, pressing the sweet tight peaks of her nipples against thin silk, he thought he'd die of wanting her.

With a tortured oath he fell back on the bed. "Leave," he croaked in a guttural command and flung an arm over his eyes. "Leave now, or so help me, Scarlett, we'll both regret it."

Time passed in fragments of silence and sound. The hushed rustle of watery silk against the smooth, tanned satin of her skin as she walked hesitantly across the varnished oak floor toward the door. A gust of wind splattered the rain against the window. A ghostly creak of protest from ancient door hinges. A long humming moment, before the finality of her decision to leave him, was punctuated by the fit of the door to the jamb and the click of the latch bolt slipping home.

Thunder rolled. Regret eclipsed any feelings of relief as he dragged in a ragged breath, let it out... then opened his eyes in disbelief when the sigh of silk drifted across the room from the closed door.

He lifted his arm and saw her standing there. Watching him. Waiting for him to say the word that would sanction her decision to stay and bring her to his side.

"Scarlett. This would be so wrong for you."

Shattered pride, searing need. He saw it all on her face as she took the first step that led her to his bed.

"How can something that feels so right be wrong?"

With a groan he tore his gaze from hers. He couldn't look at her searching eyes without wanting to touch her. He couldn't breathe without wanting to be inside her.

"You're asking the wrong man. I'm not the one who's going to end up hurt. I'm not the one who's going to be left here with my regret and yours for company."

"Regret," she echoed with such poignant entreaty he physically felt her need. "Yes, I'll probably regret it if we make love. But it will be nothing compared to the regret I'll have if we don't.''

He swallowed hard and turned back to her. She was beside him now. So close he could see her pulse beat at the hollow of her throat. So close he could smell the fragrance of her shampoo.

She eased a hip onto the bed beside him. Her slight weight and the sudden contact stole his breath. Her heat seeped through the fabric of his slacks to his skin. The burn was like liquid lightning, searing his blood, arching to his groin.

"It's been so long," she confessed in a voice made plaintive with need and husky with desire. "I want... I want to feel like a woman again. I want to know what it feels like to be wanted for something other than—'' her voice broke before she managed a wavery smile "—than my good cooking and my hospitality.

"I'm not asking for promises, Colin. I know you're going to leave. It's okay. I'm not asking for anything but this moment."

More than when she'd first entered the room, he saw the measure of her vulnerability. The asking was hard for her. The denial was killing him. Still, he gave it one more try.

"I don't want to hurt you."

She blinked hard. Looked at the hands folded tightly together on her lap. Met his eyes again. "The only way you could hurt me is if you turned me away."

He'd been looking for an excuse. She'd just given it to him. And in that moment he hated himself for his weakness.

"If I was half the man I ought to be, I'd have convinced you to be gone by now. But I can't fight this. Not any longer. I want you too much. I have from the beginning.''

Relief. Anticipation. Desire. He saw everything she was feeling through her eyes. Everything but the one thing that should be there. Regret.

Tomorrow she'd be sorry. But not today. Today he wouldn't give her anything to be sorry for. Today he'd give her everything he could as a man.

He held out his hand. Hers was trembling when she placed it in his and let him pull her down to his side.

''So what do you say,'' he whispered, in a weak attempt to ease the tension that was suddenly as thick as the storm riding on the air. ''Should we try to figure out a way to make two wrongs into a right?''

She nestled against his heat. Trusting. Compliant. Electric with the energy of expectancy. ''I say if anyone can do it, we can.''

With a tenderness he'd never felt for a woman, he raised himself on an elbow and looked into her eyes. ''You'll tell me...what you like...what you don't like. What I can do to please you.''

Her breath was shivery with anticipation. Her smile as fragile as crystal. ''Something tells me you already know.''

She was right. He did know. He told her as much when he lowered his head to hers and took her sweet mouth the way he'd been aching to take it since he'd first tasted her that night in the dark. Any lingering fantasy that he could play the white knight and send her away, faded to black with that kiss. He became totally immersed, completely involved in the wonder and the wealth of her responses.

Scarlett sank into his kiss, surrendered to his seduction and the deep, drugging possession of his mouth. His body above hers was hot and strong, pressing her into the mattress, moving in compelling enticement against her.

She ran her hands along the sleek muscle of his back, reveling in the feel of him beneath her fingers, the slight trembling of his arms that spoke of his bid for control.

His mouth was amazingly soft, achingly gentle as he scattered a string of nipping, claiming kisses along her jaw.

"I've dreamed of this." He raised his head, looking into her eyes as his hand forayed lower to glide along the inside of her thigh. "I've dreamed of you coming to me in red silk and sweet heat. I've dreamed of you beneath me—I've imagined you above me," he whispered and, with a groan of need, shifted and lifted until he was on his back and she was straddling his hips.

She caught her breath, braced her palms on his chest as he reached between them and undid his pants. Shoving them roughly down his legs, he kicked them free.

"Do you have any idea how beautiful you are? No," he said, reacting to the slight, shy shake of her head. "I don't think you do.

"Look," he prompted, turning his head to the mirrored dresser by the bed. "Look at yourself. See why you've been driving me out of my mind with wanting you."

Slowly she did as he asked. She turned her head toward the antique dresser. The mirror was wavy with age, the silvering faded with time. The images caught in its reflection seemed locked, somehow, in another place and era.

Spellbound, she saw the woman and the man together. She knew it was them but felt removed from the picture, somehow—but not from the sensual pleasures his body beneath hers fostered.

The woman in the mirror was wanton and lush. Her cheeks were fired with desire. Her hair, a tumble of red-gold curls, fell seductively over one eye. Tangled and riding high on her thighs, her red silk robe was held in place only by the sash at her waist and the sleeves slipping in soft folds down her arms.

The lapels were parted, baring breasts that were full and proud, flesh the color of ivory, nipples of rose velvet.

"No...don't look away," Colin softly commanded when she tore her gaze from the erotic sight. "Look. See how we look together."

Mesmerized by the huskiness and the heat in his voice, she did as he asked. A shiver of sensual need sluiced through her as she met his silver eyes in the mirror. A shudder of carnal anticipation had her arching her back as he raised his hands, tugged her sash free and, inch by calculated inch, pushed the robe fully open for the pleasure of his gaze—and the touch of his hands.

He was right. It was beautiful seeing them together this way. The contrasts were stunning. He was lean strength and bronze muscle. She was soft curves and pliant flesh. His hands were wide, his fingers long as they closed over her breasts and cupped them in his palms. Her hands were small, her fingers fine-boned and delicate as they covered his and she leaned into his kneading touch.

She asked him with the rocking rhythm of her hips, the caress of her hands over his to pleasure her, to love her, to do what he would to ease the ache spreading deep and low inside her.

The heat and length of him nestled against that secret, moist place between her thighs. She dug her knees deeper into the mattress on either side of his hips and pressed herself against him.

With a muffled oath, he reared up in the bed, clasped her ribs in his broad hands and sought her breast with his mouth. He found a nipple and surrounded it, sucking hard, tugging harder, voracious in his passion, greedy in his need.

She cried out, stunned by his intensity. Loving it, feeding it with the press of her breast to his mouth, she knotted her hands in his hair and rocked her hips deeper against his arousal.

He wrenched his mouth away on a ragged groan. "Sweet heaven," he murmured, nuzzling his mouth between her breasts. "You steal a man's control."

With a touch of her hand to his jaw, she tipped his face to hers. "This isn't about control. This is about what we feel...what we need. And right now I don't need your control. I need you. Please...please Colin," she whispered against his mouth. "Please—"

He cut off her plea with the crush of his mouth as he lifted her and, laying her with her head at the foot of the bed, pressed her to her back beneath him.

He didn't ask where the condom came from. He didn't even take the time to appreciate her foresight. Instead, he tore it from her hand, ripped it open and sheathed himself.

And then he was inside her. Filling her, stroking liquid velvet and sleek, tight heat. He couldn't get deep enough. Couldn't go slow enough to savor and satisfy this insatiable need to possess and pleasure this woman who had become a wanton at his touch.

She threw her arms over her head, gripped the iron foot rail with her hands and braced herself against the thrust of his body. With each pump of his hips she lifted to him. With each withdrawal, she whispered his name and enticed him back with the lushness of her body and the sultry sweep of her lashes.

She brought him to climax with a speed that transcended any experience he'd ever known. The rush was dizzying. The force devastating. It swept over him like a flash fire. Shot through him like the lightning that crackled through the air and set it alive with sizzle and sound.

Beneath him, her lips parted by the force of her cry, she reached the summit with him. Through a haze of consuming pleasure, he watched the sensuous drift of her lashes, was aware of the glorious arch of her back, the white-knuckled grip of her fingers on black iron. Of her trembling, of her sighs. And he knew...even before the last exquisite ripple of release rolled through him, even as she held him deep and snug inside her, he knew he had to have her again.

She awoke to the sound of thunder. A distant, rumbling farewell as the storm rolled on to the north, leaving a mellow, cleansing breeze in its wake.

She awoke to the touch of a man. A slow, sensual stroke of callused palm to bare breast that said not goodbye but hello. Hello again, I'm not through pleasing you yet.

"Good." A sated murmur in her ear. "You're awake."

"Ummm."

A deep, sexy chuckle.

It was too good. Too rich. The sweet friction of his hand on her skin. The gentle tug of his thumb and finger at her nipple. The heat of his breath as his mouth replaced his hand and he made languid, delicious love to her breast.

As pampered as a cat, she stretched, then moaned in sensual abandon as his mouth forayed lower, a gentle nip at the base of her ribs, a lingering kiss at the hollow of her belly.

She raised her head and, through eyes heavy with arousal and electric with anticipation, met his gaze. With a sweep of his dark lashes, he looked up the length of her body. His gray eyes were slumberous and sure, as, watching her face, he dragged his tongue along her hip point and slipped his hand between her thighs.

With a shivery groan, she parted for him, opened for him, then came apart for him as he loved her with his mouth until tears leaked from her eyes and she was crying his name in sensation-induced desperation.

For long moments afterward, he held her. While she trembled and cried and finally laughed self-consciously at her shattering response to his loving.

"You were beautiful," he insisted, stroking a hand along the length of her back.

She sniffled into the hollow of his throat. "I was out of control."

He smiled against her temple. "And then some."

She managed a lazy chuckle. "You're sounding way too pleased with yourself."

"Ummm."

She pushed up on an elbow. Dragging a handful of

hair away from her face, she smiled into his laughing eyes. "Somebody's going to have to put you in your place."

"Ummm?"

"I think, the sooner the better."

With an aggression she'd never been confident enough to display, even during the years when her marriage had been good, she proceeded to wipe that cocksure smile off his face—and replace it with one of sheer, unadulterated exhaustion.

Eight

When she awoke again, it was to the light of the oil lamp burning in the window. She sat up slowly and groaned when her body reminded her she'd stretched muscles in ways they hadn't been stretched in many, many years.

Raking her hair away from her face, she searched the room...and came up empty. She eased carefully off the bed, found her robe on the floor and, still cinching it around her waist, tiptoed barefoot down the back stairs.

She found him in the kitchen. When he spotted her, his face broke into a smile that turned her knees to noodles.

"Hi," he said, walking toward her.

"Hi, yourself," she returned shyly, and let him pull her into his arms.

"I thought you were going to sleep through until morning."

"What...? And leave you to fend for yourself? You must be hungry."

A dangerous light danced in his eyes. "For many things."

She couldn't help it. She blushed.

He couldn't help it. He laughed, then squeezed her hard before letting her go and returning to the counter.

She leaned a shoulder against the wall, content to simply watch him. He'd pulled on his pants, but nothing more. Bare-chested and barefoot, and breathtakingly beautiful, he moved around her kitchen with the sureness of a man who knew exactly what he wanted to accomplish.

"What are you up to?"

"I'm fixing your dinner," he said with a roguish grin.

"*You're* fixing *my* dinner? Haven't you got the roles reversed, here? I'm the innkeeper. I should be—"

"You should be sitting," he said, promptly walking toward her. He swept her up in his arms and deposited her on the counter with a deliberateness that left no opening for debate. "It's time, Ms. Morgan, that someone saw to your needs for a change."

"But—"

"No buts," he said, and, reading the protest in her eyes, faced off with her. He made a place for himself between her thighs and cupped her face in his palms. "You can fuss till the lake runs dry, but frankly, Scarlett, I don't give a damn."

She smiled, feeling sappy, silly and completely enamored with this extraordinary man. "You've been waiting for a chance to deliver that line haven't you?"

He kissed her quick and hard. "Sometimes my originality astounds me," he said with a deadpan grin. They both knew she'd heard that line a hundred times.

You astound me, too, she told him with her eyes. If not for his originality, for his charm and for being the sweetest, most selfless, most exciting lover a woman could hope for.

"You've got a little explaining to do Miz Scarlett."

His expression had suddenly turned so serious, she frowned. "Explaining?"

"How does a charming, chaste innkeeper, just happen to have—" he reached into the pocket of her robe and pulled out a foil packet "—these so handy?"

"Oh. Those," she said with a self-conscious little smile.

"Yeah, those." Tucking the packet into his hip pocket, he draped his wrists over her shoulders as his scowl transformed to a teasing grin.

"We do have a honeymoon suite, you know."

"And?"

"And it was occupied a week ago."

He tilted his head. Interest danced in his eyes. Amusement colored his voice. "Well now, that really is original. Instead of chocolates or flowers on the pillows, you provide complimentary condoms."

She rolled her eyes. "Not quite. I checked the room first thing in the morning after they left, before I'd even gotten dressed...just in case they missed something when they packed."

"Just in case?"

"Well I do have a teenage daughter. When I found

them, I pocketed them before she cleaned the room. I guess I forgot about them.''

"Until today.''

"Until today.''

"Lucky for us you remembered in the nick of time.'' He dipped his head and smiled into her eyes. "You're very pretty when you blush.''

"You're really enjoying this, aren't you?''

"What I'm enjoying is you.'' To prove it, he kissed her again, long and slow and savoring, before he went back to the business of their dinner.

And as she sat there, watching him prepare salads and take secret peeks into the oven, she let something happen that she knew was the mistake of her life.

She let herself fall in love. Let herself admit that from the beginning she'd felt much more than a physical attraction for this man. Made herself accept that until the end—which for him was little more than a week away, but for her would extend into forever— she would love him.

With a bittersweet longing, she indulged in his attention as he served her in the dining room and charmed her over candlelight and wine. With an ache in her heart, she let him feed her strawberries and whipped cream and lost herself in the sweetness of his kiss when he licked the juice from her lips.

She made herself laugh and play and pretend it wouldn't end, as she convinced him he needed her help with the dishes that turned into a soapsuds fight. She luxuriated in every nuance of attention, saved every precious memory, savored the richness of his loving, when he took her again to his bed.

In the tender hours before morning, she rose slowly and curled up in a chair across the room. For a long time she sat there, watching him sleep, limned in a ribbon of moonlight that washed in through the window. Watched him stretch and sprawl over the bed in all his golden glory. Listened to the sound of his breathing and, unaware of the tear trickling down her cheek, thought of the loneliness that would come when he was gone.

Morning dawned sunny and warm. After a shared shower that turned into another steamy session of lovemaking that sent them back to bed to recuperate, they decided to forgo their morning run and instead, hike to the falls. Colin, equipped with a backpack Scarlett had filled with a picnic lunch, let her lead the way.

The forest was lush and green after the rain. She pointed out dozens of wildflowers, naming them, praising them, asking, didn't he agree this was just about the prettiest place on earth?

He smiled and agreed. And felt the guilt settle in.

She was trying too hard. She smiled too much. She laughed a little too quickly. He knew the reason. She was already regretting that they'd crossed the line. She was preparing herself for his leaving. And all the while he was trying to come up with excuses to stay…at least for a little while longer. An extra week. Maybe two.

With a muffled oath, he nixed the thought. He couldn't stay. They'd both known it from the onset. He had a business to get back to. He had his life to get back to. And she had hers to get on with.

"Is this fantastic or what?"

He'd been so engrossed in the futility of his thoughts, he hadn't realized they'd reached the top of the cliffs. Neither had he been aware of the increased volume of the sound of rushing water.

He crossed the few yards toward her and saw then what she was so taken with. On the other side of the rise, in all its wild, rolling glory, Crimson Falls spilled in a froth of white foam and rippling red water over the cliffs to the lake, five hundred feet below.

And yes, it was fantastic.

So was she.

Backlit by sunshine and an iridescent, arching rainbow that shimmered in the mist from the falls, she looked breathless and vital. And so beautiful that he felt the effect of her smile in ways he couldn't catalogue or define. No woman had ever touched him as deeply as this one had. No woman had ever moved him as completely.

"Can you imagine anyone wanting to desecrate this beauty with roads and power lines and condominiums?"

He didn't want to talk about roads or power lines or condos. But he didn't want to talk about his feelings, either. They were too strong. Too intense. Too real. And totally futile. He was going to leave here. He was going to leave her.

He didn't want to talk about that, either. He couldn't bear to see the sparkle leave her eyes or to spoil the time they had left together.

So he opted for the coward's way out.

"You know, don't you, that the condos could be good for your own business? Wait—" He held up a hand to stall her quick and fiery comeback. "A road would make it more accessible. The condos would make it visible. The more exposure you get, the more business—"

"This isn't about business," she insisted, impatient with his logic even though they both knew it was sound. "This is about principles. And preservation. It's about bucking progress in favor of the past."

"All valid arguments...but you're one woman, and the odds are against you."

"And that means I should just fold?"

"No," he said softly, admiring her determination in spite of it all. "It doesn't mean you should fold. It means you need to be prepared for something you might not like...and be ready to take advantage of it."

She looked toward the falls and away from him. "I don't think I want to argue about this. Not today."

Not today because it was their last day. Their one and only day alone together before Casey, Geezer and the new guests arrived back at the hotel.

"I don't want to argue, either," he said, and shrugged off the backpack.

When she just stood there, staring at her beloved falls, he decided to try on the idea from her point of view. "Where, exactly do they want to build them?"

She turned to him, judged his intent and must have realized he was coming from a different angle. "Up there." She pointed toward the far ridge to the right of the waterfalls. "Right beside them. You wouldn't be able to look at them without staring smack into barbecue grills, tubular lawn furniture and striped umbrellas."

Hands on his hips, he surveyed the land with a scowl. "Looks like it would take some major earth moving to get a road up there."

"Not to mention a loss of trees. That's one of the last stands of virgin forest in the state. Do you realize how rare it is to find original-growth trees in this day? Mutilating it would not only be a sin against nature, it would be an abomination against man."

He couldn't help it. He grinned at her unwavering vehemence. "You got a soapbox to go with that speech, Miz Scarlett?"

She wheeled on him, ready to tangle, until she recognized the teasing challenge in his eyes. "You damn betcha, city boy. And I plan on using it day after tomorrow at the public hearing."

"Public hearing?"

"The company behind the development plan has to get county approval before they'll be able to build. Until they do, the whole project is on hold. I'm not the only one against this. Abel and Mackenzie, J.D. and Maggie, to name a few. If enough of us speak out, if our arguments are sound, we might be able to end it before it begins."

"I hear a lot of *ifs* in there."

She looked back at the falls. "We're bucking economics. As is the case of most county governments, the coffers can always use more cash. Unfortunately, money talks louder than sentiment or even posterity…as in preserving Legend Lake and Crimson Falls for our generation and the ones to come."

"Who's the developer, and how did they get ahold of the property in the first place? I thought this was mostly state park and national forest up here."

"Mostly, yes. But this particular land tract was homesteaded by a man named Swen Iverson close to a hundred years ago. It's remained in his family ever since. Several years ago when the state wanted access to expand the park, his heirs refused to deed it over. Now, however, with the dollars this Dreamscape Corporation is shelling out, the family has agreed to sell.''

"Dreamscape? I don't think I've heard of it.''

She dropped to her knees, unzipped the pack and started unloading their lunch. "It's a company out of the Twin Cities. They've been trying to buy property up here for years to develop as getaways for die-hard business types. You know, workaholics who need to be force-fed rest and relaxation and clean air before they overdose on money and power.''

Her sneaky little slam stole the last of the tension between them. He reached for the blanket and helped her spread it across the ground. "Should I be taking offense at that remark?''

She broke into a wry grin. "If the stress level fits—''

"Has it ever been suggested, Ms. Morgan,'' he said, easing down beside her, "that you have a nasty little mouth on you?''

"That's not what you said last night.'' Her coy smile had him reaching for her. "Or this morning,'' she managed between giggles when he pinned her beneath him with a feigned leer.

"That mouth is going to get you in trouble.''

"I think that it already has,'' she murmured, as he touched his lips to hers and made them both forget all about Dreamscape and his imminent departure— and gave her all the trouble she could ever want.

They lazed the day away making love, making fun, making memories Scarlett would treasure long after he left and the winter cold turned the crystal blue waters to the silver gray of his eyes.

And later, with the picnic blanket again and a bottle

of wine, they shared the last night they'd have alone together on the widow's walk overlooking the lake.

"I don't think I've ever seen a sky so crowded with stars." Colin lay on his back, staring with the awe of discovery.

Beside him, Scarlett shared his wonder with a smile. "If I'm reading that faint hint of color edging in on the horizon correctly, I don't think the light show's over yet."

"Light show?"

"Aurora borealis."

He turned his head to look at her, before averting his gaze back to the sky. "Northern lights? No kidding. I didn't think we were far enough north. Or in the right season."

"Up here you never know. We catch glimpses of them on and off all winter and occasionally in summer, too, if the conditions are right."

As they lay there, the sky gradually transformed from inky black to shades of pearly gray, then ascending hues of blue and lavender with streaks of red and green flashing across the whole like bold brush strokes over canvas.

"What makes it happen?"

"Depends on who you ask. Mackenzie insists they're the work of an ancient Chippewa magic man."

"First, ghosts. Now, magic."

"As I said, that's Mackenzie's version, not mine."

"And Maggie—does she have an explanation too? And don't say ghosts."

She returned his lazy smile. "Nope. She says J.D. has convinced her that something as romantic as the northern lights shouldn't be questioned. They should simply be enjoyed for the miracle they are.''

"What about Scarlett Morgan," he asked softly. "What does she believe?"

She turned to him. The tenderness in his eyes touched her so deeply she had to look away. She'd like to believe in the magic of the Chippewa legend and call on it to find a way to keep Colin at her side through a thousand more nights filled with northern lights. She'd like to believe in romance as the means to the end she wanted, but knew it would never be enough.

Blinking back the tears that were trying to escape, she purposely broke the spell. "I believe it's the walrus," she said matter of factly.

"Walrus?" He practically laughed the word.

"Yup," she confirmed, reacting to the grin in his voice, grateful her little bit of silliness had ended the mood. "According to Geezer—"

He snorted. "Makes sense this would come from Geezer."

"According to Geezer," she persisted, ignoring his skepticism, "an old legend in some Eskimo tribes is that the colored bands are spirits of the dead, playing ball with a walrus skull—or, vice versa—that the walrus spirits are playing with a human skull."

He shook his head. "Sorry. Walrus just don't do it for me. I think I'll have to go along with J.D. on this one and opt for romance."

The moment he'd said it, they both realized the implication of his words. He was a man who didn't look for, or want, love in his life. He was a man who had priorities, and romance wasn't one of them.

Yet as he lay beside her, watching the sky dance

with color and clarity, Colin questioned again the va-
lidity of his life choices to date. Just as he questioned
if he really had it in him to leave her here and walk
away.

Suddenly he had a need to know more about her—
and no inclination to stop himself from asking.

He turned on his side, propping his cheek in his
palm. The curve of her waist was slender and supple
as he caressed her there, satisfying his need to touch
her. "What happened to your marriage, Scarlett?"

He knew he had no right to ask. And for a moment,
as she took the time to react to his unexpected question, he thought she'd tell him as much.

Instead, with a softly reflective tone and carefully
chosen words, she answered with a dismissive shrug.

"The same thing that happens to many marriages,
I guess. We were too young. Too focused on individual needs. Too stupid to know what to do about it.
The stress finally got the best of us and we parted
ways."

Well. That was neat and tidy. Too neat. Too tidy.
And she was too tense. There was more to the story.
He knew he shouldn't, but he pressed. "That's it?"

She let out a deep breath, gave another one of those
evasive shrugs. "Pretty much."

"Do you ever hear from him?"

For the first time her control slipped. The smile that
tipped up her lips was bitter. "Once…maybe twice a
year he calls to talk to Casey. Usually to apologize
for missing her birthday or to explain why her Christ-
mas gifts were late or why he didn't make it to his
parents when she was there visiting. He's always got
some deal going. Some big venture, simmering on the

back burner, that's turned out to be more important than her."

"Casey's a sweet kid," he said, unable to curb the anger in his voice. "She deserves better. You deserved better, too."

She said nothing.

"Do you still love him?"

Silence had never been so loud as he waited, denying that a negative reply was as important as his next breath.

"I'm not sure I ever loved him," she said at last, and he told himself the regret he heard was due more to circumstance than sorrow.

"I was infatuated with him in the beginning. Charmed by him even. But it never developed into love. If it had, I would have fought harder to keep the marriage intact. In the end, though, I gave up trying even for Casey's sake."

"You left him."

She nodded. Not pleased. Not proud. Just resigned.

"And he didn't try to stop you?"

"I wouldn't go as far as to say that."

"Then he wasn't a total fool." It was on the tip of his tongue to say that a man would have to be a fool not to fight for her. A bigger fool to walk away.

Just as he was planning to do.

"John fought everything," she said, breaking into his regrets but not destroying them. "His problem was, he fought for all the wrong reasons."

She turned to him then, her dark eyes concealing secrets he knew she was withholding, even as she searched his for answers. "Why are we talking about this? Casey comes home tomorrow. Geezer, too, along with a number of reservations. This is our last night together, Colin. I don't want to spend any more of it talking about what's past."

He didn't want to let it go. He didn't want to let her go, either. But he had no hold on her past and no rights in her future.

What he had was tonight and half a dozen tomorrows, when he would share her company but not her bed before he left her life and went back to his.

"Tell me what you want," he whispered, drawing her against him, the promise implicit in his embrace that whatever she wanted he would deliver.

She didn't tell him. She showed him. With the passion of her kiss and the desperation of her lovemaking. There on the widow's walk, beneath the vastness of the Minnesota sky and the exotic dance of the northern lights, she took him inside her and gave him everything she was as a woman. She made love to him as if it were the first time, as if it were the last time...as if she were saying goodbye.

"You been up t' no good, ain't ya?"

It was the night after Casey and Geezer had returned to Crimson Falls. It was the night after he'd made love with Scarlett on the widow's walk and felt her come apart in his arms.

Colin was standing on the dock, contemplating the night, trying to void the memories the two of them had made together.

Geezer's voice was a jarring reminder of those things he was trying to forget.

He turned toward the sound of the old man's shuffling gate, squinted through the darkness and saw him standing at the base of the dock.

"While I was gone," he continued, his tone accusatory, "and you was alone here with her. You couldn't keep them hands t' yerself. I knew I shouldn'a left her by herself with the likes a' you."

Colin figured he deserved the dressing down, though Geezer couldn't add anything to what he'd already told himself a thousand times.

He turned back to his study of the lake, letting the night sounds and the water sounds drown out Geezer's mutterings and the guilt he was already heaping on himself.

Scarlett hadn't told Colin the public hearing on the condo issue was being held in the hotel. Had he thought about it, he would have seen the logic. What better place to plead for the preservation of the past and the land than in the midst of it?

The dining room was as full as he'd seen it since he'd been here. Several locals had boated over to show support for one side or the other. Some of the hotel's new arrivals had even wandered in to see what was going on.

The Greenes had been among the first to arrive and, in a show of solidarity for Scarlett's cause, were sharing a table with Colin and Casey and Geezer. The Hazzards arrived late. When Colin saw J.D. and Maggie slip inside, he sent J.D. a look across the room.

J.D., undaunted by Colin's "I've got a bone to pick with you" glare, gave Colin a huge grin and a thumbs-up.

Colin just shook his head. James Dean Hazzard was a difficult man to dislike—let alone hold a grudge against. Still, Colin was about to give him a dressing down, when Scarlett took the floor.

The crowd stilled as she eloquently and passionately stated her case. Everyone listened, but it was to a handful of government officials and a contingent of Dreamscape attorneys and company reps that she spoke.

"She's on a roll now."

This from Casey who had returned from the Greenes yesterday morning early enough that Colin and Scarlett had had to scramble out of bed and hustle around to look presentable—and platonic.

On that issue Scarlett was adamant. "Casey is not to know or suspect what went on here while she was gone. She's missed having a male influence in her life. I don't want her to get the wrong idea about us."

As the day progressed, he spent it regretting the end of their intimacy and the lost chance to make lazy morning love to her one more time, and he wondered just what idea Casey might get if she knew.

Would she get the idea that he was in love with her mother? Would she see, as he sat there this very moment with his hands suddenly wrapped around his coffee cup in a white-knuckled grip, that he'd just figured out *that* was exactly the case?

He was in love. For the first time in his life he was in love. The impact of that unthinkable truth hit him like a lead pipe.

Stunned, he sat there, watching the woman who'd breached a barrier he'd thought impenetrable, and accepted that he'd been in love with her from the beginning. He couldn't imagine that there was a drug made, legal or otherwise, as potent as the feelings she evoked in him—or as mind-bending. Hell of a pill to swallow for a man who had an aversion to something even as benign as aspirin.

After only one day of generic smiles, forced, distant courtesy, and one long, empty night without her in his arms, he already felt the loss. He just hadn't realized it was love he was losing. Hadn't realized, as he'd lain awake half the night coming up with and then tearing apart ideas to stretch their time together, that it was love he was trying to keep intact.

Well, he knew it now.

He was still struggling with the newness and the disbelief when the room erupted into an enthusiastic round of applause. Only then did he realize she'd spoken her piece. And only when she made her way through the crowd to take a seat beside him at the table did he realize that walking away from her was going to be one of the hardest things he'd ever done.

Nine

"Well, now we wait." Mackenzie took a sip of iced tea and, with an encouraging smile for Scarlett, fell as silent as everyone else in the room.

They were in the dining room: the Greenes, the Hazzards, Colin and Scarlett. It was late afternoon. The crowd had slowly disbursed after the round-robin session of open-mike comments and arguments that J.D. and Mackenzie had added to Scarlett's. Some of the others had spoken, too—both for and against the advent of the condos. The county officials had listened patiently to all. Only when the representatives from Dreamscape spoke, however, with their graphs and charts and carefully illustrated drawings and dollar signs, did they show any reaction. That reaction had been *greed*.

Everyone at the table knew the power of the dollar and its ability to win over sentiment and ideals.

"'A tree hugger,'" Scarlett sputtered, staring glumly out the window toward the falls. "That pompous, placating opportunist actually called me a tree hugger. Tried to make me out as some militant environmental activist who was more wrapped up in cause than purpose."

"Well, there's one thing about it," Maggie added, sympathetic with Scarlett's disgust, "he didn't make any points taking that tack. Everyone who knows you knows how ridiculous that label is."

"Regardless," J.D. added, playing devil's advocate. "He planted the seed in the minds of the decision makers, and now that it's planted it'll grow."

"Just like the tax revenues, if the project proceeds. Hey, don't glare at me," Colin protested, when all three women shot daggers in his direction. "I'm just stating the obvious. Money is the lowest common denominator. I'm sorry, but the way I see it, money is going to decide the issue."

"Unfortunately, Colin is probably right." Typically, Abel had been silent up until this point. Also typically, when he spoke people listened to what he said. "You did what you could, Scarlett. Maybe we'll get lucky and it will be enough."

But they all feared it wouldn't be.

"You think she's going to be okay?" J.D. asked, as Colin walked with him and Abel to the lakeshore. Maggie and Mackenzie strolled along behind with Scarlett. Casey and Mark, along with Nashata and Hershey and the puppies, were far ahead of them as the strung-out procession made its way to the dock where the Hazzards' float plane and the Greenes' boat were moored.

Colin shoved his hands deeper into his pockets and shrugged. "With the probable decision? No. Can she handle it? Yeah. She's a survivor."

"Didn't I tell you she was one special lady?"

Colin made sure the women were out of earshot. "You know, Hazzard, I ought to rearrange that pretty face of yours for the meddling you've done in our lives."

Beside them, Abel chuckled. "Sorry. I was just remembering having some thoughts of my own in that direction at one point."

"I am wounded. Truly wounded that either of you would think I'd meddl—"

"Stow it," both Colin and Abel said in unison, which prompted an involuntary grin from all three of them.

"So...what's the plan, Stan?" J.D. asked, cutting right to the heart of the issue.

Colin angled him a look.

"Oh, come on. I see the way you two look at each other. What I want to know is what are you going to do about it?"

It was useless to deny it, pointless to protest.

"There's nothing I can do," Colin said honestly.

"What are you talking about? One look at you together and anyone can see you two were made for each other."

Colin avoided J.D.'s probing stare. "It's complicated."

"And your point is?" J.D. prompted, his tone implying *Life is complicated, deal with it.*

"My point is, we're compatible, but our lives aren't."

"So find a way to compromise. Figure it out, man. She'd make a beautiful bride."

Colin snorted. "And here I gave you some credit for subtlety."

"Think about it," J.D. advised sagely, all nonsense gone from his tone. "Think about what you'd be giving up if you let her go.

"Besides," he added, when the tension threatened to take over. "I want to be able to come back again without living in fear of Scarlett taking after me with one of her kitchen knives."

"Her knives are the least of your worries, pal. The lady has far-less-civilized plans for dealing with you. The only reason she didn't carry them out today was her preoccupation with the condo issue."

While he'd been silent during their discourse, Abel's mouth twisted into that fleeting facsimile of a smile that Colin now equated to amusement.

"She'll mellow out," J.D. said with confidence. "In the meantime, there's got to be a solution for the two of you. My money's on you to figure it out."

Colin wiped the sweat from his brow with the back of his wrist and took one final swing with the ax. With a cracking sound, the dead birch fell. The thud of the trunk and the splintering of limbs as it hit the ground were at odds with the stillness of the morning, but in complete harmony with the way he felt.

He'd spent the night thinking about what J.D. had said. He was right. There ought to be a way for him and Scarlett to be together. But he'd be damned if he could come up with it.

"I don't know why you don't use the chain saw,"

Casey said from her perch on a boulder beside him. "Sure would be a lot easier. Faster, too."

Colin didn't want *easy*. He didn't want *fast*, either. What he wanted was to work himself into a state of fatigue so complete he'd sleep tonight from exhaustion.

He couldn't blame his lack of rest on Belinda's room anymore. Since the night he and Scarlett had made love, the room had been as quiet as a tomb. No shaking bed. No restless windows. No shadows dancing on the wall. And no problem getting out of the room. No more dreams.

He wasn't sure what Casey's reasons for that turn of events would be, but he knew his. He'd fixed the room with hammer and nails and a plane. He didn't need to dream because he'd lived out his fantasy.

If only he could fix his other problem as easily.

"Hello-o-o," Casey singsonged, a playful reminder that she was still there and waiting for his response. "The chain saw? Do you want me to get it?"

He shook his head. "I need the workout."

"You and my mom," she said in that way teenagers have of letting adults know that the teens would never understand what motivated them. "She can't keep busy enough. Always running. Baking this. Cleaning that. What's with you two, anyway?"

Thwack. He buried the ax in the trunk and tried to ignore her.

"I kind of had the idea you liked her," Casey persisted, hiking her knees to her chest and propping her chin on them.

Thwack.

"I was...I don't know. I guess I was wishing you

liked her a lot. She gets lonesome sometimes. She doesn't say it. But I can tell."

He stalled his swing midair then let the ax head hit the ground. "Your mom's a very special woman, Casey. And I like her just fine."

"But not enough to...you know. Make her someone important in your life."

Leave it to a child to reduce *convoluted* to *plain and simple*. "Your mom is important to me."

"So how come you always go the other way when you see her coming?"

Giving it up, he dropped to the ground beside the boulder. He leaned back on his elbows, stretched his legs out in front of him and crossed them at the ankles. Letting the lake breeze cool his brow, he stared at the toe of his shoe. "Is that how it looks?"

"That's how it looks." A long pause followed. "Is that how it is?"

Reluctantly he looked up at her, squinting against the sunlight. He saw her need to know and decided to level with her. "We have feelings for each other, Casey, but we both know they can't go anywhere."

Her face scrunched up in thought. "Because she's not a sophisticated lady?"

"No. No," he was quick to assure her. "Because we live different lives. Her life is you and the hotel. Mine is my business."

"I bet it would be different if I wasn't in the way."

Her summation was so quick, her expression so vulnerable, he was just as quick to set her straight.

"Don't even think it. You're just as special as your mother, Casey. The two of you together are a pair any man would find hard to resist."

She gave a little sniff then fussed with the frayed hem of her cutoffs. "My dad didn't find it so hard."

It took all of his control to curb his disgust with the man who ignored a child as unique as Casey. For her sake, though, he gave her father the benefit of the doubt. "Your dad probably knows by now that he made a very big mistake when he let you and your mother go."

She slipped down from the boulder and gave him a quelling look. "So how come you haven't figured out yet that you're going to do the very same thing?"

With that insightful little indictment, and a last, soulful look from her big, brown eyes, she walked away.

It was that look that made him sit up and take notice. That look and her straightforward assessment. Why *was* he going to walk away? Because he was so sure Scarlett wouldn't go with him? Or because he was afraid to find out that she would?

He'd never thought of permanency with a woman. Never contemplated commitment of the forever kind.

But then, he'd never been in love. And he'd never had a woman like Scarlett at stake. Maybe it was time he listened to what Hazzard and Casey and his heart were trying to tell him.

"Come with me."

Startled, Scarlett jumped at the sound of Colin's voice. She startled at just about everything these past few days. Shadows. Memories. Regrets.

How long had it been since she'd had a full night's sleep? Since making love with him. Since the hearing.

It felt like a month instead of just a few days.

Putting on her best face, she turned away from the

stove and the bread she was baking to see him standing just inside the doorway. His arms were crossed over his chest. One shoulder was propped oh so casually against the doorjamb. Only his expression, serious and pensive, betrayed the intensity he'd brought with him into the room.

"How long have you been standing there?" she asked, and fought her heart's reaction to go to him. He looked so beautiful, so serious, so much the man she loved and had worked so hard to avoid.

"Come with me, Scarlett," he said again, his face somber, his eyes searching.

She tried for a throwaway smile. "I'm in the middle of preparing dinner. I can't go anywhere right now."

His jaw clenched with impatience. "I'm not talking about right now, this very minute. I'm talking about five days from now when I leave." A long, thick silence passed. "I want you to come with me."

Stunned, her forced smile collapsed. She searched his face, her heart running haywire, her mind spinning a hundred revolutions a second, and struggled to comprehend the significance of the request he was making.

Before she could catch her breath, or gather her thoughts, he was beside her, his hands on her shoulders, staring deep into her eyes.

"Come with me. You and Casey."

She covered shock with panic. "Colin...we can't go anywhere right now. The hotel—I've got guests. I've got several bookings coming in next week. I've got—"

"Forget about the hotel. We'll find someone to

take care of it. Think about yourself for a change. Think about what you want. What you need.''

What she wanted was Colin. What she needed was to remember that she couldn't have him. ''Colin, I don't know what to say. This…this is really special that you'd invite us to…to visit, but I can't leave my business.''

He pulled her closer. ''I'm not asking you to come to visit,'' he growled. Import laced through every word.

With the same passion that he'd held her, he let her go. He paced to the back kitchen door, dragged a hand through his hair, then whirled on her again.

''Do you need to hear the words? Can you possibly not know what I'm asking?''

She blinked once…twice. Then, in defense against an avalanche of emotions, she answered his questions with denial. ''No. I don't know what you're asking. I'm not sure you do, either,'' she added, softly challenging him.

When he swore under his breath and didn't deny it, she sensed she'd hit on the truth.

Her already battered heart broke a little more—this time for him. How she loved this kind, caring man who was trying to do the right thing, but wasn't yet sure of his reasons.

''Scarlett…I've never asked a woman to share my life. I've never even come close.''

''Don't,'' she whispered, but with such urgency he stopped and listened. She couldn't bear to hear him say any more. Couldn't bear to live with the knowledge once he went away. ''Don't say something you'll be sorry for. Don't start something else we can't finish.''

She turned away from him so he wouldn't see the tears brimming. Driven by the conviction that she was right, and the fear that she'd give in if he pressed her, she made herself hold the line.

"I can't go with you. I can't leave here—not with so much to be done. Crimson Falls is my home. New York is yours. I wouldn't fit in there, and I couldn't ask you to live here. You wouldn't be content. We've both known that from the beginning. And we've both known what we shared couldn't last."

She flinched when he came up behind her, resting his hands lightly on her shoulders. "Couldn't we at least try to figure out a way to make it work?"

His voice was a caress. A promise to please. A plea to bend.

"Please," she begged, more sharply than she'd intended. But she was running scared, and she had to make him see. "Please don't say any more. And if you care anything about me, you won't bring it up again."

He was still standing there when she all but ran out of the kitchen, away from him, away from the wanting, but not away from the tears she'd tried so hard to keep at bay.

He'd blown it. He wasn't sure yet how, he just knew he had. At first he'd felt defeated. Now he was just plain mad. At himself for botching it. At her for running away. But he wasn't about to give up without a fight.

By the next evening, fueled by conviction, driven by excitement, and with the help of the shortwave radio and a conversation with Abel Greene, everything was in place.

Everything but confronting Scarlett with what he'd done. He knew the fur was about to fly when he saw her storming down the path to the lake toward him.

Braced with his arguments, he waited for her there.

"Would you mind telling me what this is about?" she demanded, waving a sheet of paper under his nose.

Undaunted, he cast a sideways glance at the paper and shrugged. "It's a little order I placed."

"A little order? There are several thousand dollars worth of materials listed here. I can't afford to pay for this! And whatever made you think you had the right to order it in the first place?"

He'd known she'd be angry. He'd known she'd have to work it through. What he hadn't known was that he'd feel so guilty over his heavy-handedness, but he hadn't seen any other way. She was one proud, headstrong woman. If he'd asked if he could do this for her, she'd have nixed the idea in a heartbeat.

"First, you don't have to pay for it," he said reasonably. "I'm footing the bill. And second, winning the raffle gives me the right. In case you've forgotten, I am part owner."

She stared, her expression incredulous, and he knew he hadn't made any points reminding her of that bit of fact.

"Part owner, yes. Emphasis on *part*," she pointed out hotly. "A small one. One raffle ticket at a thousand dollars hardly gives you the right to make these kind of decisions."

"No, those rights don't come with one ticket." He waited a beat, then lobbed his little bomb. "But forty tickets should count for something more than a passing interest."

He waited, watching her carefully. Her face went as white as chalk.

"You...bought forty tickets?" Much more than surprise made her breathless. There was panic in the question, panic and a desperate wanting to not believe what she'd just heard. "Why would you do that?" She stared at him as if he were some kind of a monster. "Why would you spend money like that on something you didn't need and didn't know anything about? Why would you buy every ticket?"

One word hit him with the impact of a sledge. "What do you mean—*every* ticket? I bought forty, not all eighty."

"Eighty? There weren't eighty tickets."

A sickening sense of foreboding stuck in his throat like sludge. "Not according to J.D. He said he'd sold the first forty and wheedled me into buying the last forty so he could call it a wrap."

Even before the words were out, he knew Hazzard had nailed him again.

The shock on her face had turned to denial, denial, to stunned defeat. "There were no other tickets." Her voice sounded hollow and weak. "J.D. wanted to sell eighty thousand dollars worth but I drew the line at forty. I couldn't bring myself to do more. I felt like I was selling my soul as it was."

She met his eyes again, this time with a wistful, wild desperation. "You really bought *every* ticket?"

He would have lied and told her no if he thought it would strip the anguish from her eyes. But it was too late for lies and too late to change things. "Apparently."

She clutched a hand to her throat, looked despairingly toward the hotel. "Well...what does it matter now? Congratulations, Colin." She met his eyes with a look of defeat so devastating he physically felt her pain. "It looks like I'm working for you now."

"What are you talking about?"

"I'm talking about the fact that Crimson Falls is more yours than mine. Your forty thousand dollars is more than I've got paid off on the mortgage."

With a moisture glistening in her eyes that did strange, tugging things inside his chest, she turned to go.

"Scarlett, wait."

"For what? For you to tell me more about how things are going to be run around here with you in charge? For you to call some more shots?"

"I don't have any intention of taking over."

"No? That's not what this is telling me." She shoved the list of materials against his chest.

"You don't understand," he insisted, staying her with a hand on her arm when she whirled away. "I did this for you. I did it for us. I want Crimson Falls to be everything you want it to be, so that you don't have to worry about it any more.

"Scarlett, you work too hard. You deserve to be cared for. We can hire someone to help you run the hotel."

"I don't want to hire someone to run the hotel. The hotel is mine. Or it was." With a determination that was a physical effort, she blinked back tears. "But that's not the only issue. Are you and your money so removed from the real world that you can't see what's important here? It's not just about me. It's not just about the hotel. If I don't stay here and fight, Dreamscape won't just move in, they'll take over."

He shook his head sadly. "You're one small woman. You can't fight everything."

"I can try." Pride fired her eyes.

"To the exclusion of all else?"

She fell silent. She looked scared. And confused. And very, very weary.

"You can't win this one, Scarlett. I think you know that. And I think you're fighting me because you know you can't win the other battle. Don't do it. Don't fight us. Come with me to New York."

"You know that can't happen."

"Only because you won't let it. We can work something out. We could live between New York and here. There'd be no reason why it wouldn't work."

Scarlett had quit listening. She was still stunned by, and mired in, the realization that with his investment in Crimson Falls, she'd lost controlling interest.

"You don't understand," she said wearily.

"Then help me. Help me to understand. I thought I was doing something that would please you. I thought I was providing a solution."

"A solution? Your solution was to defeat me? Well, you've done exactly that. Not only do I feel defeated, I feel diminished. For the second time in my life, I've been reduced to dependence on a man to make my decisions for me."

Stunned, for a moment all he could do was stare. "That's how you see this?"

"That's what it is. You ordered the materials. You decided what was best for me....

"No, thank you. I had a bellyful of having my life run for me when I was married to John. I came here to get away from that. I came here to prove to myself that I'm strong enough to make my way on my own.

And I was doing just that—until you and your forty thousand dollars just took it all away from me.''

Finally he understood the depth of her despair. He'd known there was more to the breakup of their marriage than she'd let on. Now he knew what the undefined factor was. Her ex must have had a real power trip going, and she'd been a casualty.

Somehow he had to make her see this was different. "I wasn't taking, Scarlett. I was giving."

She shook her head adamantly. "No. You were controlling. I won't let that happen to me again. I don't want your help. I don't want your interference. I don't want you making decisions for me, and I don't want you running my life." The fire in her voice turned to ice. So did the look in her eyes. "Do you understand?"

"Yeah," he said, after a long, considering moment. "I think I do. Another man took away your independence, and I'm paying the price."

A tear slowly leaked from one eye. "You paid the price all right. I hope it was worth the money."

He didn't stop her when she turned away this time. He couldn't do anything but stand there and watch her go. And know that what he'd hoped would bring them to common ground had only succeeded in widening the gap. Widening, hell. There was no way he could ever reach her now.

Ten

During the night Colin decided there was nothing left to do but leave. It wasn't what he wanted. It wasn't what she needed. But she was going to have to come to that conclusion by herself.

He'd radioed J.D. at the crack of dawn and ordered him to fly over and pick him up, no questions asked. A few minutes ago he'd heard the float plane circle the bay and knew J.D. was taxiing up to the dock as he carried his luggage down the stairs.

Casey was all sad eyes and deep sighs as she stood just inside the lobby door. In silence she watched him set his bags on the floor.

"Where's your mom?"

Casey cast her eyes downward and hiked her chin toward the kitchen. "She's making chocolate chip cookies."

He watched her in silence, dreading the moment

when he would walk in there and tell Scarlett good-bye. It was hard enough telling her daughter.

"She only makes chocolate chip cookies when she's really sad," Casey added, unaware that she'd just ground a little more salt into some very raw wounds.

He jammed his fists into his pockets and stared at his feet. "I'm afraid I'm responsible for that. I blew it, Casey. I hurt her bad. I never meant to."

"Then tell her." Her dark eyes, so much like her mother's, brimmed with tears.

He shook his head. "She doesn't want to hear it. And until she does, I'm just wasting my breath."

"Does that mean you're coming back?"

He cupped his palm behind his nape, wishing he hadn't heard so much hope in her question. "I don't know what it means. I only know I've got to get out of here and put some distance between us. I've got a lot of thinking to do. She does, too."

She crossed her arms over her chest and gave him a lost puppy look. "She's going to miss you. Me, too."

Those eyes of hers could melt candle wax. "Yeah, well, that goes both ways." He hesitated only a moment, then opened his arms to her. "Come here, squirt."

She threw herself against his chest in a heartbeat, her tears leaving damp tracks on his shirt. A thick knot of emotion clogged his throat as he held her.

"I was going to teach you how to swim," she said between sniffles, and his heart broke into a thousand little pieces.

"Yeah, well, I don't know if either of us were up

for that little adventure. Rocks don't float, and I've got a feeling I don't, either."

That little bit of nonsense finally earned him a grin. He squeezed her shoulders and set her away.

"Take care of your mother, okay?"

She nodded glumly.

With one final, reassuring squeeze of her arm, he walked toward the kitchen.

The sweet scent of fresh-baked cookies greeted him when he opened the door. The sight of Scarlett, beautifully mussed and valiantly busy, was almost more than he could handle.

She acknowledged his presence in the room with a quick look, before slipping on an oven mitt and pulling a sheet of cookies out of the oven.

"I came to say goodbye." It hurt to say the words. Just like it hurt to look at her and know it might be for the last time.

She stalled for an instant before resuming her motions like an automaton. Slip the spatula under a cookie, slide it from the sheet, settle it onto a cooling rack. Start all over again.

He waited in silence, watched as her movements slowed, then stopped altogether. And still she didn't look his way. She just stood there, her head down, her eyes closed, and, he suspected, her heart breaking like the pieces that were left of his.

"I'd ask you again to come with me, but I don't think I could take another hit like the last one."

Silence. Thick. Conclusive.

For a long moment he stood there, debating the wisdom of what he was about to say. In the end, wisdom didn't factor in. What he felt for her did.

"I know you don't want to hear this, but I'm going

to say it, anyway. I love you, Scarlett." Once he'd admitted it aloud, the rest of the words were automatic. "I wanted to make the rest of my life with you. But I guess that's not going to happen, is it? Not as long as you feel I'm guilty of the same crimes as your ex-husband."

He paused, his chest tight with regret, as a single tear spilled onto the counter and landed on her tightly clenched fingers.

"I'm not him, Scarlett. And the only thing I'm guilty of is trying too hard to make it work between us. I didn't want to control you. I wanted to love you. I messed up. And I'm sorry. Looks like I'll always be sorry."

The tremulous rise and fall of her shoulders was the only response she gave him. It wasn't enough to keep him there. Which meant it was time to go.

"Don't worry about the hotel. Abel will see to the renovations. Any changes you want made in the plans, talk to him."

It never happened. That moment he'd been waiting for when she'd turn to him, open her arms and forgive him. But he couldn't just leave. Not without touching her one last time.

He crossed slowly to her side. Slower still, he raised a hand to her face, brushed a fiery red-gold curl away from her cheek and pressed a soft kiss there.

With the sweet scent of her hair filling his senses, the petal softness of her skin already a memory on his lips, he turned and walked out of her life.

"What do you think it means?"

Scarlett turned at the sound of Casey's voice. She

was standing just inside the door of Belinda's room. Leaning against the doorjamb, she stared at the oil lamp burning at low wick. "I was just wondering the same thing."

Every night since Colin had left two weeks ago, when she'd climbed the stairs to go to bed, she'd found the door standing open, the oil lamp on the table by the window lit.

She crossed the room, feeling the memories she and Colin had made here surround her like a warm blanket. Bending to the lamp, she softly blew out the flame, knowing as she did that it would be burning again when she got up in the morning.

"I think she's waiting for him to come back."

The wistful look in her daughter's eyes tore at Scarlett's heart. She'd been unusually quiet since Colin had left. Guilt hit her hard and fast. She'd been so mired in her own misery that she hadn't realized until this moment how much his leaving had affected Casey.

"Well, she's wasting her time and my lamp oil," she said, attempting to lighten the mood. Her heart wasn't in it, though, and Casey knew it.

"You could ask him to come back."

"Oh, honey. If only it was that simple."

"It is. It *is* that simple. All you have to do is do it."

Feeling far older than she was, she sat down on the edge of the bed and made a place for Casey beside her. "Come here."

Head down, Casey joined her. Scarlett draped her arm over Casey's shoulders and hugged her tight.

"You liked Colin a lot, didn't you?"

"He was a nice guy. He said he messed things up

between you guys. He said he told you he was sorry. Why can't you tell him it's okay?''

That was the question of the hour. Every hour. Every day. Every night since she'd let him walk away. ''I don't know,'' she finally said honestly. ''I'm afraid, I guess.''

''Of Colin?''

She withdrew her arm and folded her hands together on her lap. ''I guess you could say that. I'm afraid of how I feel about him. I'm afraid of his success. His self-assurance. I'm afraid he'll swallow me up, and somewhere along the way I'll lose who I am.'' She smiled crookedly. ''Does that make any sense to you? If it does, let me know and you can help me figure it out.''

''Do you love him?''

She smiled again to keep back the tears. '''Fraid so.''

Casey's frown was deep and perplexed. ''If you love him, why did you let him go?'' With a look that said she would never understand adults, she left her.

Left her alone in the room where she and Colin had made love. Left her alone with her regrets and a love so strong it hurt. Left her with Casey's question echoing through her mind—the very question she'd asked herself a thousand times.

If you love him, why did you let him go?

Everything had changed. Everything he'd valued. Everything he'd stood for. Everything that had been important.

He'd been back in the city for two weeks. He couldn't look out the tinted plate-glass windows to the concrete city below and not think of a forest full of trees. He couldn't walk down the street full of the chaotic sounds and smells of the city and not remember the silence, the bird song and the cleansing scent of fresh air and pine.

He couldn't go to bed at night and not see Scarlett beside him, her summer-tanned skin, her lush, giving body, her smile of sheer feminine seduction beneath the dance of the northern lights.

"Colin?"

He turned to his brother's voice. Cameron was standing beside him in his office, a file folder in his hand.

"What?"

"The Black project? We were talking about cost overruns? Hello? You're here in body, but where the hell is your mind?"

Colin turned back toward the window. "Just figure it out. You don't need me to pin it down."

"This from Mr. Hands-On-at-All-Costs? What happened to you out there in the great, wild North, anyway? You lose your 'control' gene in the woods?"

Control. There was that word again. The one Scarlett had thrown in his face. The one he'd seen as a strength, not a weakness—until it had cost him her.

"Just do it, Cam, and quit giving me grief."

"I don't think I have a single thing to do with your grief. You want to tell me who does?"

Colin worked his jaw and kept his silence.

"It's a woman, isn't it?" Cameron said after a long moment, his tone ringing with surprise and discovery. "Well, I'll be damned. Big brother's finally been bitten by the love bug."

"You're pressing your luck here."

"And it's well worth the risk. Hot damn. I never thought it would happen. So who is she, and why isn't she here?"

Colin turned to him with a glare that could have flash-frozen fire.

"What? She turn you down? Ah." He narrowed his eyes when Colin's silence confirmed yet one more conclusion. "She turned you down. Amazing."

"I'm not in the mood."

"This is news? You haven't been in the mood for much more than brooding ever since you came back early I might add."

"Will you just get this over with and leave me alone?"

"It's not up to me to do anything here. You're the one who needs to either get on with things or get over them. Hey, man," Cameron added, not only as his brother but his friend. "Fix it. It's what you do."

Fix it. It's what you do.

Cameron's words hung in the room long after he'd left it. They stuck in his mind for days afterward. So simple. So concise. He fixed worn-out buildings and made them new again. He'd repeatedly done the impossible and become successful in the process.

So why hadn't he been able to fix what had gone wrong between him and Scarlett?

It was several days later when frustration had driven him out of the office and into the field. They'd bought a condemned apartment building for a song last month. Reconstruction had started last week. He'd donned hard hat and work boots and was in the midst of concrete dust and chunks of debris when he sensed he wasn't alone.

Snagging a kerchief from his hip pocket, he wiped the grime from his face, then, sensing again that he was being watched, slowly turned around.

Dust filtered through the air in layers of soft powder. Sunlight backlit and shone in refracted rays on his brother and the small frame of a woman wearing a hard hat by his side.

His first reaction was anger. Cameron knew better than to bring someone other than crew onto a work site. He whipped off his hat and stalked toward them—then stopped dead in his tracks when he recognized the red-gold of the curls peaking out from under the formed plastic helmet.

He blinked, then blinked again, finally accepting that it was Scarlett standing there, tentative, self-conscious, beautiful.

Cam gave him a thumbs-up signal over Scarlett's head, mouthed the words "Fix it," and made himself scarce.

And still he just stood there, conscious of the sun on his back, the sweat trickling down his temple, the elevated rhythm of his heart.

"So," she said, taking a hesitant step toward him, "this is how the money man makes his money."

Watching her, he pulled off his leather gloves, then his hat, and tossed the gloves inside it. "You're a long ways from home."

"Yeah, well…someone very important to me invited me to come to New York a while back. I decided to see if the invitation was still open."

He tucked the hat under his arm and watched her carefully. "I'm not so sure it was such a good idea—accepting the invitation, that is."

"No?" she said, more sigh than sound, and he saw the panic in her eyes.

"Actually, the city isn't the greatest place to be this time of year. I was thinking—I was hoping—that someone...someone very special to me, would invite me to this wonderful old hotel she runs near the most beautiful waterfall in the world."

The relief in her eyes eased the ache in his chest. The tears that followed nearly sent him to his knees.

"I've missed you Miz Scarlett," he said, barely getting the words past the lump in his throat as he reached for her, then folded her against him when she launched herself into his arms.

To touch him again was heaven. To feel him inside her where he belonged, the sweetest thrill she'd ever known. To drift off to sleep in his arms, safe, secure, well loved, was unlike any pleasure she'd ever encountered.

"Are you awake?"

His husky murmur near her ear stirred the hair at her nape. She drew his arm tighter around her and turned on her back so she could see his face.

They were in his bed. In his apartment. In deep, complete love.

Shadows played across his cheeks in the darkness. Candlelight flickered in the lazy drift of his eyes.

"I love you," she whispered.

"And," he prompted, a soft smile tilting his lips.

She lowered her lashes. "And you're nothing like him."

He tipped her face to his with a curled finger under her chin. His smile had faded, but not his gentleness.

"Tell me. Tell me so I'll know to never make the same mistakes he did."

She drew in a deep breath, struggling with how to say what she needed to say. Finally she just started talking and hoped that when she was through he would understand.

"I'm not sure he made any mistakes." Her statement was met by silence but she pressed on. "I think I'm the one who made them. I let him have control over me. I don't even know how it happened. One day I was this young, eager-to-please bride—then somewhere along the way, that's all I was doing. Pleasing. Or at least I was trying to. I'm not making any sense, am I?"

He stroked his thumb along her jaw. "Keep working on it. You'll get there."

"I think I did it to myself. I wanted our marriage to be as good as my parents' marriage was. Only I didn't realize then that theirs was, and is, a give-and-take arrangement. I turned ours into I gave and he took. I set myself up for it. In retrospect I can't even blame him for taking advantage. After all, if someone lays down a rug, you walk on it."

She stopped, drew a deep breath, then snuggled into the warmth he offered.

"It was like he was pushing me to see how much control he actually had. The old 'jump when I say jump and ask how high on the way up,' trick. And I let it happen. By the time I wised up, it was too late. He'd lost his respect for me, and I'd lost my respect for myself. Everything deteriorated from that point on."

She paused and drew a deep breath before continuing. "When I walked out, he was so stunned that

I'd found a backbone again, and so used to having the final word, he refused to grant the divorce.''

"What finally convinced him?''

"I did. Me and my newfound sense of self. The mouse became the shrew, and he didn't much care for me that way.''

"Good strategy,'' he said, giving her a quick hug.

"It wasn't strategy. It was me at the end of my rope. And believe me, I was not a nice person right then. But I was stronger. And it was the strength that got me through it—and back to the person I wanted to be.''

"Independent. Self-reliant.''

"Yes. It was hard, but I did it. And then you came along. You and your sexy eyes and sultry smile and your charm and your money and your power—''

"And you saw the reel running all over again.''

She nodded against his chest. "Yeah.''

"So what did *I* do? I start throwing my money around, taking things out of your hands. All the savvy of a rhino.''

She smiled at the self-disgust in his voice. "And all the charm of a—''

"Televangelist?'' he prompted.

This time she chuckled. "All the charm of the most desirable, the most magnetic, the most selfless lover a woman could ever want.''

He was quiet for a long moment. "I was coming back, you know. If you hadn't shown up here, I was coming back. To make amends. To make you see I never wanted to control you.''

"I finally figured that out,'' she whispered against his chest. "If I hadn't been so crazy in love with you and so certain it couldn't work out, I would have realized sooner."

"Realized what?"

"What motivated you," she said without hesitation. "I finally realized you weren't motivated by any need other than to see to mine. I finally realized," she continued, easing up on an elbow so she could look down into his eyes, "that what you did, you did because you loved me, because you cared about me, and you were trying to find a way for us to be together, instead of positioning yourself for control."

"I do love you," he murmured, drawing her down to his chest. "But since you mentioned position, let's talk about it." He smiled into her eyes and moved his hips suggestively against hers. "And control," which was suddenly hers when she matched his actions with her hips. "Lord. Do you have any idea the kind of control you have over me?"

"I don't want to control you." She opened her legs at his urging and eased down over his heat. "I want to love you. And love you," she murmured, her breath mingling with his as he penetrated, slow, and hot, and deep.

Epilogue

"Scarlett, are you up here?"

When she didn't answer, Colin poked his head through the hotel's attic door and looked inside.

Filtered sunshine poured in through the dormer window, sending dust motes dancing in beams of slanted light.

"Scarlett," he called her name again and, ducking a cobweb, walked into the room.

"Over here."

He followed the sound of her voice, curious as to the pensiveness of her tone. "Maggie said you were up here." He dropped down on his haunches beside her, where she knelt on the floor, the musty contents of an old trunk spread out around her. "What are you doing?"

"It's hers," she said, holding a fragile length of red silk in her hands.

"Hers?"

"Belinda's. Look." She rose to her feet taking the silk with her, then holding it out for him to see. "It's her red dress."

They'd been back at the hotel for three weeks, and he'd long since stopped fighting both Scarlett's and Casey's convictions about Belinda.

He told himself it was because he was humoring them, but there were times—like now—when he came close to feeling what he suspected the ladies in his life felt. A presence. A purpose. A sense of restless need.

He touched the dress's flowing hem with his fingertips. "Why are you so sure it's hers?"

"This." She reached into the trunk and carefully pulled out a picture. After studying it for a moment, she handed it to him.

It was an old tintype of a woman. A beautiful, voluptuous woman wearing a flowing silk gown. The same gown Scarlett held with such awe in her hands.

"Turn it over. Read what's written on the back."

"'Belinda Jackson,'" he read aloud. "'1909.'" He looked from the picture to the dress, before he met her eyes. "Not much of a legacy, is it?"

She smiled sadly. "She made her own legacy. Maybe we now can put it to rest."

When they came downstairs, the kitchen was a beehive of activity. Maggie and Mackenzie were busy baking the wedding cake. J.D. and Abel were good-naturedly sputtering that they'd never factored "florist" into their résumés as they hung garlands of flowers from the cornices above the dining room windows.

Casey and Mark were down by the lake giving Hershey and Nashata and the puppies baths for the special occasion. Geezer, ever his ebullient self, sat in a rocker on the verandah, regaling both Colin's and Scarlett's parents with tales of the lake, stories about the hotel and the fact that he'd pegged Colin as a worthy match for Scarlett first off.

Cameron met them at the bottom of the stairs. Yesterday, he'd helped Colin set up his office—complete with fax, phone, modem and assorted other technological marvels that would assist him in running Slater Corporation from the hotel when he and Scarlett were in residence. After being gone from the place for almost a month, and realizing how much he'd grown to appreciate the serenity, Colin already knew they'd spend more time here than he'd anticipated. Still he looked forward to sharing New York with Scarlett and Casey.

"Hey you two," Cameron said with an amused grin, "we thought you'd decided to start the honeymoon a little early. Where've you been?"

"A gentleman wouldn't ask," Colin advised him, tucking Scarlett under his arm.

"Just like a gentleman wouldn't tell," Scarlett added, leaning into his embrace.

"I like your friends," Cameron said, as they walked into the dining room where J.D. was singing "Blue Moon" and Abel was stoically tolerating it.

"I'd like to say J.D.'s not usually so—"

"Obnoxious?" Colin supplied deadpan.

"Well, there is that," Scarlett said with a grin, to which J.D. strongly objected from his perch on a ladder. "I was going to say lyrical. But ever since he found out—"

"Ever since I found out I'm going to be a daddy," J.D. crowed with a grin of pure, pompous pride that changed to one of stunning love and affection when Maggie walked into the room, "I just can't stop singing," he finished, and burst into "Maybe Baby."

"I'm afraid this child is going to be born tone deaf." A radiant Maggie gave her husband an indulgent look that told everyone in the room J.D. could mutilate "Rock-a-bye Baby," and he'd still sound like Sinatra to her ears.

"You," Abel barked, climbing down from the other ladder to relieve a very pregnant Mackenzie of a full grocery sack as she waddled into the room. "Will you use a little sense?"

"Will you relax, Daddy?" Mackenzie shook her head at Abel's proprietary attention. "There's nothing in the sack but table napkins."

"See what you have to look forward to, Scarlett?" Maggie and Mackenzie asked in unison, then hooked pinkies with a giggle to seal their parallel thoughts.

"Is there something you haven't told us, dear?"

All heads turned to see Scarlett's mother, Elizabeth, standing in the dining room doorway, a hopeful light in her eyes.

"No, ma'am," Colin said when he realized Scarlett was too stunned to respond. "Our friends are anticipating, that's all. And that's how rumors get started." He sent an admonishing grin to the culprits, before reassuring Scarlett's mother. "If and when we decide to add to the family, you'll be the first to know."

"And we *will* discuss it," Scarlett said, stalling a smile. "Especially if I'm going to have to put up with solicitation and songs for nine months."

"No way," Colin assured her with a look that said

he'd never act as foolishly as J.D. and Abel—who promptly exchanged "We'll see" grins.

"But I hope you realize, baby or no baby, I plan on spoiling you and Casey rotten."

"I think I can deal with that," Scarlett said, after pretending to consider.

"Good." He pulled an envelope out of his shirt pocket. "Then you can start by dealing with this."

She looked from him to the envelope with expectant curiosity.

"A gift for my bride."

Her eyes telling him she would love it, whatever was inside, she opened the envelope and drew out the paper.

"Oh." Her hands began to shake when she realized what she held. "Oh, my. It...it's..." Her eyes glittered with tears of stunned disbelief.

"It's the deed to Iverson's land," Colin finished for her. "Crimson Falls is yours now, Scarlett. You don't have to worry about anyone tearing up the forest or building anywhere near it ever again."

"How?" was all she managed as she clutched the precious deed to her breast.

He shrugged, caressing her face with his gaze. "Let's just say I made Iverson a better offer than Dreamscape."

"But I thought they'd sealed the deal as soon as the council gave approval for the project."

"Well, *they* thought it was going to happen that way, too. I guess I was more persuasive."

Tears still brimming in her eyes, she moved into his arms. "I've noticed that about you." Then to the delight of everyone in the room, she showed him with her kiss exactly how much she loved him.

* * *

She came to him in silk. Belinda's silk. Shimmery red. Slipping softly off her shoulders. Parting slightly to show a smooth length of tanned leg. The flowers she carried matched the ones in her hair. Only the scent of her skin rivaled their fragrance.

She became his bride by the Crimson Falls she treasured.

With the moon holding council to the gathering of family and friends, and the northern lights dancing across the night sky in breathtaking rainbow hues, she pledged her love, for life, and he pledged his life forever.

And when everyone else had called it a night, he carried her up the stairs to Belinda's room—where the shadows had ceased to dance on the walls, and the oil lamp no longer burned on the table by the window.

* * * * *

Coming this July...

36 HOURS

Fast paced, dramatic, compelling... and most of all, passionate!

For the residents of Grand Springs, Colorado, the storm-induced blackout was just the beginning. Suddenly the mayor was dead, a bride was missing, a baby needed a home and a handsome stranger needed his memory. And on top of everything, twelve couples were about to find each other and embark on a once-in-a-lifetime love. No wonder they said it was 36 Hours that changed *everything!*

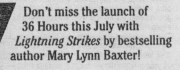

Don't miss the launch of 36 Hours this July with *Lightning Strikes* by bestselling author Mary Lynn Baxter!

Win a framed print of the entire 36 Hours artwork! See details in book.

Available at your favorite retail outlet.

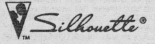

Look us up on-line at: http://www.romance.net

36IBC-R

MILLION DOLLAR SWEEPSTAKES
OFFICIAL RULES
NO PURCHASE NECESSARY TO ENTER

1. To enter, follow the directions published. Method of entry may vary. For eligibility, entries must be received no later than March 31, 1998. No liability is assumed for printing errors, lost, late, non-delivered or misdirected entries.

   To determine winners, the sweepstakes numbers assigned to submitted entries will be compared against a list of randomly, preselected prize winning numbers. In the event all prizes are not claimed via the return of prize winning numbers, random drawings will be held from among all other entries received to award unclaimed prizes.

2. Prize winners will be determined no later than June 30, 1998. Selection of winning numbers and random drawings are under the supervision of D. L. Blair, Inc., an independent judging organization whose decisions are final. Limit: one prize to a family or organization. No substitution will be made for any prize, except as offered. Taxes and duties on all prizes are the sole responsibility of winners. Winners will be notified by mail. Odds of winning are determined by the number of eligible entries distributed and received.

3. Sweepstakes open to residents of the U.S. (except Puerto Rico), Canada and Europe who are 18 years of age or older, except employees and immediate family members of Torstar Corp., D. L. Blair, Inc., their affiliates, subsidiaries, and all other agencies, entities, and persons connected with the use, marketing or conduct of this sweepstakes. All applicable laws and regulations apply. Sweepstakes offer void wherever prohibited by law. Any litigation within the province of Quebec respecting the conduct and awarding of a prize in this sweepstakes must be submitted to the Régie des alcools, des courses et des jeux. In order to win a prize, residents of Canada will be required to correctly answer a time-limited arithmetical skill-testing question to be administered by mail.

4. Winners of major prizes (Grand through Fourth) will be obligated to sign and return an Affidavit of Eligibility and Release of Liability within 30 days of notification. In the event of non-compliance within this time period or if a prize is returned as undeliverable, D. L. Blair, Inc. may at its sole discretion, award that prize to an alternate winner. By acceptance of their prize, winners consent to use of their names, photographs or other likeness for purposes of advertising, trade and promotion on behalf of Torstar Corp., its affiliates and subsidiaries, without further compensation unless prohibited by law. Torstar Corp. and D. L. Blair, Inc., their affiliates and subsidiaries are not responsible for errors in printing of sweepstakes and prize winning numbers. In the event a duplication of a prize winning number occurs, a random drawing will be held from among all entries received with that prize winning number to award that prize.

5. This sweepstakes is presented by Torstar Corp., its subsidiaries and affiliates in conjunction with book, merchandise and/or product offerings. The number of prizes to be awarded and their value are as follows: Grand Prize — $1,000,000 (payable at $33,333.33 a year for 30 years); First Prize — $50,000; Second Prize — $10,000; Third Prize — $5,000; 3 Fourth Prizes — $1,000 each; 10 Fifth Prizes — $250 each; 1,000 Sixth Prizes — $10 each. Values of all prizes are in U.S. currency. Prizes in each level will be presented in different creative executions, including various currencies, vehicles, merchandise and travel. Any presentation of a prize level in a currency other than U.S. currency represents an approximate equivalent to the U.S. currency prize for that level, at that time. Prize winners will have the opportunity of selecting any prize offered for that level; however, the actual non U.S. currency equivalent prize if offered and selected, shall be awarded at the exchange rate existing at 3:00 P.M. New York time on March 31, 1998. A travel prize option, if offered and selected by winner, must be completed within 12 months of selection and is subject to: traveling companion(s) completing and returning of a Release of Liability prior to travel; and hotel and flight accommodations availability. For a current list of all prize options offered within prize levels, send a self-addressed, stamped envelope (WA residents need not affix postage) to: MILLION DOLLAR SWEEPSTAKES Prize Options, P.O. Box 4456, Blair, NE 68009-4456, USA.

6. For a list of prize winners (available after July 31, 1998) send a separate, stamped, self-addressed envelope to: MILLION DOLLAR SWEEPSTAKES Winners, P.O. Box 4459, Blair, NE 68009-4459, USA.

SWP-FEB97

**This summer, the legend
continues in Jacobsville**

Diana Palmer

A LONG, TALL
TEXAN SUMMER

Three **BRAND-NEW** short stories

This summer, Silhouette brings readers a special
collection for Diana Palmer's LONG, TALL TEXANS
fans. Diana has rounded up three **BRAND-NEW**
stories of love Texas-style, all set in Jacobsville,
Texas. Featuring the men you've grown to love from
this wonderful town, this collection is a must-have
for all fans!

*They grow 'em tall in the saddle in Texas—and
they've got love and marriage on their minds!*

Don't miss this collection of original Long, Tall Texans
stories...available in June at your favorite retail outlet.

Look us up on-line at: http://www.romance.net   LTTST

And the Winner Is...
You!

...when you pick up these great titles
from our new promotion at your
favorite retail outlet this June!

Diana Palmer
The Case of the Mesmerizing Boss

Betty Neels
The Convenient Wife

Annette Broadrick
Irresistible

Emma Darcy
A Wedding to Remember

Rachel Lee
Lost Warriors

Marie Ferrarella
Father Goose

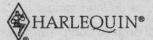 

Look us up on-line at: http://www.romance.net   ATWI397-R

New York Times **Bestselling Author**

REBECCA BRANDEWYNE

FOR GOOD OR FOR EVIL—
THE INSIDE STORY...

The noble Hampton family, with its legacy of sin and
scandal, suffers the ultimate tragedy: the ruthless murder
of one of its own.

There are only two people who can unravel the case—

JAKE SERINGO is the cynical cop who grew up on the
mean streets of life;

CLAIRE CONNELLY is the beautiful but aloof broadcast
journalist.

They'd parted years ago on explosive terms—now they
are on the trail of a bizarre and shocking family secret
that could topple a dynasty.

GLORY SEEKERS

The search begins at your favorite
retail outlet in June 1997.

MIRA The brightest star in women's fiction

Look us up on-line at: http://www.romance.net   MRBGS

HARLEQUIN ULTIMATE GUIDES™

HAVE A LOVE AFFAIR WITH YOUR KITCHEN...
ALL OVER AGAIN!

Get great tips from great chefs! Find out how to:
- get the best produce
- create the most enticing meals
- cut preparation time
- set a table guaranteed to make 'em go WOW!
- turn culinary disasters into triumphant cuisine

Want to be the star of every meal? Then you'll have to find out

What Great Chefs Know That You Don't

Available in June, at your favorite
Harlequin/Silhouette retail outlet.

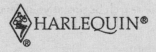

Look us up on-line at: http://www.romance.net

CHEFS

National Bestselling Author

JOANN ROSS

does it again with

NO REGRETS

Molly chose God, Lena searched for love and Tessa
wanted fame. Three sisters, torn apart by tragedy,
chose different paths...until fate and one man
reunited them. But when tragedy strikes again,
can the surviving sisters choose happiness...with
no regrets?

Available July 1997 at your favorite retail outlet.

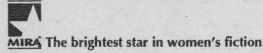

MIRA The brightest star in women's fiction

MJRNR

Look us up on-line at: http://www.romance.net

New York Times Bestselling Authors

JENNIFER BLAKE
JANET DAILEY
ELIZABETH GAGE

Three *New York Times* bestselling authors bring you three
very sensuous, contemporary love stories—all centered
around one magical night!

It is a warm, spring night and masquerading as legendary
lovers, the elite of New Orleans society have come to
celebrate the twenty-fifth anniversary of the Duchaise
masquerade ball. But amidst the beauty, music and revelry,
some of the world's most legendary lovers are in trouble....

Come midnight at this year's Duchaise ball, passion and
scandal will be...

Unmasked

Revealed at your favorite retail outlet in July 1997.

MIRA The brightest star in women's fiction

Look us up on-line at: http://www.romance.net

MANTHOL